CW00428489

# NACHES TRAIL

## McCAIN CRONICLES
### BOOK FOUR

## B.N. RUNDELL

WOLFPACK
PUBLISHING
— EST 2013 —

**Naches Trail**
Paperback Edition
Copyright © 2023 B.N. Rundell

Wolfpack Publishing
9850 S. Maryland Parkway, Suite A-5 #323
Las Vegas, Nevada 89183

wolfpackpublishing.com

This book is a work of fiction. Any references to historical events, real people or real places are used fictitiously. Other names, characters, places and events are products of the author's imagination, and any resemblance to actual events, places or persons, living or dead, is entirely coincidental.

All rights reserved. No part of this book may be reproduced by any means without the prior written consent of the publisher, other than brief quotes for reviews.

Paperback ISBN 978-1-63977-330-5
eBook ISBN 978-1-63977-329-9
LCCN 2023940437

# DEDICATION

Family—comes in all shapes, sizes, and ages, but they're still family. God gives us the gift of family and sometimes it seems like a trial more than a blessing, and sometimes just the opposite. A recent visit with several of my family, close and extended, reminded me of the preciousness of each one of them. I had to take a few moments to stop and say thanks to my heavenly Father for the gift of family. I am the youngest of seven boys, and as I write these words, I am the sole survivor of the lot. And with each one gone, every day brings reminders of times past, memories made, and words left unsaid. So, I dedicate this to my family—both my "growing-up" family and my "offspring" family—my wife and four daughters, eleven grandchildren, and three great-grandchildren. I love and treasure them all. Many thoughts expressed in my writings reflect moments spent with my family, I even named a few characters after them. I treasure each moment. I only wish I had more. So, my friends, treasure your moments, share your love and time, and make blessed memories. God bless you one and all.

# Naches Trail

# Chapter 1

## Discovery

Dusk was lowering its curtains of darkness as the eastern sky began to glow with the rising Comanche moon. The white body of the naked man tiptoed into the water that rippled with the golden hues of the moonlit night. Elijah McCain was determined to wash the stench of civilization from his tired body as it shivered with the cold water while he clutched the thick bar of lye soap in his hand, his other hand holding the LeMat pistol. He sat the pistol on the big rock that had been warmed by the sun and slowly sat down in the frigid water, his teeth beginning to chatter a familiar rhythm. He had already stripped off and washed his clothes in the light of dusk, laying them on the chokecherry bushes that sided the pool of mountain runoff. But he knew to never go unarmed, even though he had chosen to bathe by the moonlight.

His two horses, the big claybank stallion and the dapple-grey mustang, were picketed in the trees but within reach of the tall grass. His gear was stacked under a big ponderosa together with his Winchester Yellowboy rifle, the Spencer rifle, and the Colt revolver shotgun and the holstered Colt Army pistol. He did not expect trouble, but he also knew that trouble did not always come when or where expected, nor did it always come by invitation.

The cold water added a certain haste to his bathing, yet he scrubbed himself almost raw in his effort to ignore the cold in favor of cleanliness. He sudsed up his hair and whiskery face, ducked under the cold water, and came up shaking and spitting. He pushed his hair back and wiped his face of the excess water and moved closer to the big rock that shouldered up from the rippling water, casting its dim shadow into the depths of the pool. Sitting on the rock beside the LeMat pistol was a steel mirror and a straight razor that he quickly put to work on his lathered face. He twisted around to face the big moon and paused. He slowly moved the mirror about, as a figure rose from the bushes behind him.

Elijah appeared nonchalant as he moved the razor over his face, but all the while watched the figure of the boy, who appeared to be about twelve summers old, a Native, wearing buckskins, a beaded headband that held his hair back, his loose hair touching his shoulders. He held a bow with a nocked arrow before him, but the bow was not drawn, and the young man appeared to be more curious than threatening. Eli spoke just loud enough to be heard, "It's called shaving. That's what we do to remove the whiskers."

The young man jerked back, startled that he was seen, and looked about to see if there were others, beginning to bring the bow to full draw but still not aiming it at Eli.

"Yes, I can see you, but I am not here to harm you," added Eli. He sat down the razor, scooped up a handful of water to rinse his face and as he turned, he picked up the LeMat, but held it behind him as he started from the water. The boy watched, frowning, as Eli went to his stack of fresh clothes and dropped to his haunches to pick up his underdrawers, his woolen kersey britches, and linen shirt. As he dressed himself, he continued talking.

"Are you of the Palouse people?" asked Eli, looking at the young man who had not moved from his place before the bushes.

The young man pointed to himself, *"Nimíipuu!"*

Eli nodded, knowing that all Native people referred to themselves as *The People,* but that term was different in each language. "Nez Perce, huh." He slipped his shirt over his shoulders, pointed to himself, and said, "I am Elijah, or Eli." He pointed to the young warrior, "You?"

"I am *Peo Peo Tholekt,* in your tongue, *Bird Alighting.*"

Eli stomped his feet into his boots, stood as he wrapped his belt and holster around his hips and as he fastened the belt, he looked at his visitor, "Are you hungry?" using sign language to be sure he was understood. As Peo Peo nodded, Eli motioned him forward and turned to move the coffeepot and the frying pan closer to the coals of the remains of his fire, put a couple sticks on the coals, and went to his packs for the pork belly and leftover biscuits. He returned to the fire and motioned for Peo Peo to be seated and began slicing the meat into the frying pan.

Eli looked to his visitor, "Is your village near?"

Peo Peo frowned, slowly shook his head as he slipped his quiver over his shoulder and replaced the arrow, unstrung his bow and slipped it into the quiver then sat it aside, but Eli noticed the warrior's hand dropped to the haft of a sheathed knife at his side. Eli noticed the young man looking around, taking stock of this white man's camp, but he also appeared to be a little anxious, and Eli asked, "Are you looking for someone?" He continued to use sign as he spoke wanting the young man to know what was said.

Peo Peo frowned. "There are more." He held up one hand, four fingers extended.

Eli frowned. "Did something happen?"

"Our camp was attacked by white men, I was hunting. Our men," holding up two fingers, "were killed. The women were attacked and beaten. The white men left, but the women are afraid and hungry. I did not find any game for them to eat."

"Can you bring them here? I have more food and will share with you."

"You will share if I bring them?"

"Yes, I will share, and if they are hurt, I will help them. I have medicines."

Peo Peo rose, slipped his quiver over one shoulder, paused, and looked at Eli, then turned away and disappeared into the brush beside the creek. He was heard splashing across the shallow creek, and Eli caught a glimpse of his back as he slipped into the trees.

The Nez Perce were generally known as a peaceful people and Eli knew he was in the land of the Nez Perce but had not been overly concerned. There had been two treaties, 1855 and 1863, that dealt with the reduced land of the people and usually dictated peaceful ways, but Eli knew that few treaties had been honored by the white men and he had not put a lot of confidence in the treaties. Although he was fluent in some of the Native languages, the tongue of the Nez Perce was dissimilar to those of the Plains tribes.

He went to the hanging haunch of venison from the

deer he had taken the morning before and began to cut several strip steaks for his expected visitors. He returned to the fire, went to the creek, and cut several long willow withes and used them to hang the steaks over the flames to broil. He quickly whipped up some cornbread dough for biscuits and brought out the Dutch oven and sat it on some coals beside the fire, placed the biscuits in the greased bottom and replaced the lid, covering the rimmed lid with hot coals by using the big blade of his Bowie knife that was usually in a sheath at his back between his shoulder blades.

He poured himself a cup of coffee, added some water and grounds to the pot, and put it back on the rock beside the fire. He sat back, watching the trees and creek for the return of his expected visitors, but when they arrived, he was startled at the appearance of the women. They had been severely beaten and stumbled beside the two horses that carried their few belongings. Eli stood, motioning them to be seated on the log that lay just back from the fire, and he helped the women to be seated. One was middle-aged, the other younger, perhaps late teens or early twenties. Eli looked at Peo Peo as he spoke, motioning to the women. "She is my mother, Wrapped in the Clouds. She," nodding to the younger woman, "is White Bird."

The women looked at Eli with quick glances to the meat and the rest of the preparations for the meal. They looked at one another, frowning, and looked back at Eli. Wrapped in the Clouds struggled to stand, but Eli motioned for her to remain seated. "I know I'm not much of a cook, but we'll manage." He signed but got nothing but a look of confusion from the women. He pointed to the meat broiling over the flames, "You tend to those."

Wrapped in the Clouds nodded and moved from the log to her knees near the withes and looked closer to see the meat beginning to sizzle. She pointed to the Dutch oven and Eli used his big knife to lift the lid by the handle to show the women what was inside. Big eyes looked at Eli and back to the big pot, at one another and the older woman slowly shook her head as she looked at Eli. Eli chuckled, poured some coffee in two cups, and handed them to the women. As they accepted the cups, Eli held out a bag of sugar and signed for them to try some in the coffee. The women did as he said, White Bird licking her fingers and looking closer, back to Eli and smiled and nodded. When they sipped at the coffee, both women slowly lowered the cups and looked at Eli, nodding their heads and smiling.

They made short work of the meal and coffee, and the women were quick to take over as the cleanup was done. After taking the utensils and such to the creek and thoroughly washing them with the sand and water, the women chattered among themselves but were obviously pleased with the white man and his ways. When they returned, they held out the cups and Eli motioned to the packs under the tree. As they sat back on the log, Eli held out a small tin, removed the lid, and handed it to Wrapped in the Clouds. "That is medicine, made from the buds of the aspen trees. We call it Balm of Gilead." He motioned to their cuts and bruises, "Put it on the cuts and such, it will help heal."

Wrapped in the Clouds accepted the tin, lifted it close and smelled it, touched the salve with her fingers and smiled, apparently recognizing the remedy and turned to White Bird and began applying it to the worst of her injuries. White Bird did the same for Wrapped in the

Clouds as Eli turned to Peo Peo, "What happened? Why did the white men attack and why did they beat them?"

"We were camped in the trees away from the road. I was gone hunting. They said the white men rode up, shot the men. Caught the women, beat them, raped them, took two horses and our food, and rode away, laughing."

"How many and what did they look like?" asked Eli, looking to the women for the answers.

Wrapped in the Clouds snarled and spat the words as she answered Eli. "Four," holding up four fingers, "men. Hairy faces, leggings with stripes," showing stripes down the sides of their legs with her hands, "the color of your horse," pointing to the grey packhorse. "One held us down, other did what he wanted. Then changed. Dirty, smell, spit brown, dirty teeth, hurt." Anger flared in her eyes as they overflowed with tears. "They took the weapons of our men; we could do nothing."

Just listening to the description of what the men had done angered Eli. He suspected they were renegades from the war, and the color of the britches said they were Confederates. He knew there were many men from both the Union and the Confederacy that had come west in search of riches to start a new life after the war, but there would always be those that refused to work, preferring to take from others, some having learned the ways of war all too well.

# CHAPTER 2

## RESISTANCE

Eli lay in his blankets, hands clasped behind his head as he looked at the stars on this clear night when the heavenly bodies had their lanterns shining bright. He thought about those that shared his camp and what had happened to them, wondering where the renegades might have gone or what other evil they were planning. The stillness of the night prompted melancholy thoughts of his youth and the protected life he had enjoyed, even though he worked at his family's shipbuilding, it was a time of learning—values, character, compassion, commitment—words that he had learned to live by, especially the words of his father, *Do right! Always do right. Sometimes that means helping others to make things right. Son, you always have to remember, when there is evil, it can only be stopped when good men rise up against it.* Eli remembered his father saying the same thing in many different ways, but it still prompted him to stand for that which was right at every opportunity. He was never one to turn away and do nothing.

But he was on a mission, a mission to find his stepsons, Jubal and Joshua Paine, the twin boys born shortly after he married their mother, and even that was the result of making a promise to his friend and fellow West Point graduate, Ferdinand Paine, as he lay dying. Paine's wife was expecting their first child when he died and true to his promise, Elijah married her and together they raised the twin boys, although his military service kept him from home all too often. But the fulfillment of his covenant with his wife, which was given on her deathbed, was to bring her boys home, that had been his purpose in life ever since. He had traveled from their home in Kentucky to Fort Benton in Montana Territory, searching for the boys who had deserted the Union Army just before war's end and headed to the goldfields in the West. That search had taken him up the Missouri on a steamboat, down to Last Chance Gulch by Helena, Montana, and on to Virginia City, then north to Bear Gulch and Hellgate, and now he was bound to Walla Walla, Washington Territory, on the trail of a packtrain and freighters that his boys were thought to be working.

That covenant had driven him on, believing he would find the boys and tell them about their mother, and they would want to return home as she wished, but he discovered they knew about his search, and learned of his nearness, but they had intentionally left the country without any contact. So, what about that purpose? If they did not want to be found and would continue to run, should he continue? He chuckled to himself, *Of course, that's what you promised!*

And what about the rebel renegades that attacked the Nez Perce? *Do right! Always do right, remember?* He shook his head, chuckled to himself, and rolled to the side to try for some sleep, trusting his horses to keep watch and warn him of any trouble. In the distance a lone coyote cried his troubles to the moon and somewhere an owl asked his question of the night, neither receiving an answer.

A soft muzzle and a huff brought Eli fully awake. He was not startled by the movement of his horse, knowing it was his way of warning Eli and without moving, Eli searched the darkness before him as he slipped his hand around the butt of his Colt pistol that lay by his head under the edge of the blanket. Nothing moved. Eli slowly moved his head to look at Rusty, the lineback red dun stallion, to see the horse standing, head high, ears pricked and nostrils flaring. The big horse was nervous—stomping his feet, snorting, and a low rumble came from deep in his chest. Eli turned enough to look where the horse was staring and saw a flash of movement in the trees, and another, but the shadows were low to the ground and moving quickly. Eli swapped his pistol for the Winchester and brought it to his shoulder, watching the trees, and slowly came to his feet. The flash of orange eyes told Eli that wolves were trying to circle the camp, ready to attack. Eli knew the smell of smoke and man would usually keep them at bay, but the smell of meat and horse was too tempting.

Eli stood with his back to the horses, glanced quickly to the sleeping women and Peo Peo, but the young man's blankets were empty, and Eli saw the young warrior near a tree, bow in hand with an arrow nocked. Rusty snorted, jerked to the side, and Eli saw the flash of grey come from the trees, shoulder high, and fired his rifle. The flame stabbed the night, the bark of the rifle pierced the silence, and the scream of the stallion added to the cacophony as he bared teeth and lunged to meet the wolf. The bullet caught the wolf in the neck, just as Rusty's teeth grabbed at its side and ripped, tearing the fur and a chunk of hide from the dying beast.

A black shadow came from the trees, leaping toward the grey mustang, but the gelding jumped away, making the wolf hit the ground, but Eli had jacked another round into the Winchester and flame stabbed the darkness again, the bullet driving into the chest of the canine. An arrow whispered past Eli, making him turn back to the trees to see the feathered shaft drive into the chest of a grey beast, but the impact did not slow the animal's lunge, the wolf striking Eli on the shoulder, teeth grabbing at his face. Eli lifted his arm to protect his face, clinging to the rifle one-handed. The weight of the wolf drove Eli back, he stumbled and fell, the wolf snarling, snapping and growling, grabbing at his sleeve and arm. Eli dropped the rifle, now pressed between him and the wolf, and grabbed at his Bowie knife in the sheath at his back. The blade flashed in the moonlight just before he drove it deep into the wolf's chest, twisting and shoving to get the beast off, almost gutting the wolf as it fell to the side.

Eli snatched up his rifle and came to one knee, searching the pale darkness for another target. One of the women screamed and Eli turned to see a wolf attacking Wrapped in the Clouds as she covered her face and neck with an arm, kicking and screaming at the beast. Eli ran to her but could not shoot without the bullet hitting her. He lifted the rifle and brought the barrel down as a club to smash the skull of the wolf. The whine and snarl of the beast told Eli the animal had loosed his bite, and Eli drove the barrel of the rifle into the ribs of the wolf and pulled the trigger. The blast of the rifle burnt the fur and the bullet slammed through its chest taking life with it as it exited the far side in a spray of blood.

He turned, looking for other wolves, hollered at the women, "Build up the fire! We need the light!" Both women quickly grabbed wood, stacking it on the flames, but searching the trees for any attack, eyes wide with fear as they worked. The flare of flames showed movement in the trees, but the remaining wolves were retreating. Eli walked the perimeter of the camp, glancing to the women and Peo Peo and the horses to ensure all were safe. He stopped, looking into the trees by the glare of the fire, saw nothing, and went to the horses to stroke their necks and faces, talking softly to still them.

The women dragged the carcasses of the wolves to the far side of the camp away from the horses and lay them just inside the trees. When they returned, White Bird looked to Eli, "Are you hurt?"

"No, I'm alright. His teeth got my arm a little, but I'll be alright." He looked to Wrapped in the Clouds, "Were you hurt?"

She held out her arm, bloodied from the fangs of the wolf, and answered, "We have the same wounds. Where is your balm?"

"There," nodding to the saddlebags beside his saddle.

The older woman nodded to White Bird who went to the bags and fetched the tin. She sent Peo Peo for wood and water and White Bird set about tending to the wounded. The water was heated, the wounds washed, balm applied, and bandages secured. Eli felt his arm, *That's gonna be sore tomorrow!* He looked to Wrapped in the Clouds and White Bird, "Thank you."

———

THE GREY LIGHT of early morning was peeking through the trees when the women began puttering about, preparing their breakfast. Eli excused himself and with rifle in hand, disappeared into the trees. He had spotted a shoulder of stone that protruded from the trees, and he made for the rocks, intent on greeting the day in a special time with his Lord. He had also made it his practice to make a visual survey of the area before ever breaking camp and the escarpment would give a good view of the trail before him. Perhaps he could see some sign of the rebel renegades as well.

He climbed to the point of rocks, sat on a flat boulder that was crowded by a piñon, and lay his rifle at his side, the binoculars nearby, and put his Bible on his lap. The light was dim, shadows long, and the morning breeze was cool, and high overhead he heard the screech of an eagle. He searched the sky and saw the widespread wings of a golden eagle making its early morning search for a meal. The beautiful bird soared on the updraft of the mountains; his head bent down as he looked for any movement that might be tasty. Eli watched as the eagle circled, slowed, and folded his wings for a dive to a beaver pond in the creek. Sharp talons poised as he neared the surface and plucked a big trout from the waters and rose back into the sky to deliver the feast to a nest high on the skeletal tree that held the eagle's home and mate. Eli grinned, thinking about how beautiful and simple their life was, but knowing it could also turn deadly in the brief moment of a storm, a predator, or even the nearness of man.

Eli basked in the moment of the Creator's handiwork, and turned to a familiar passage and read, *But they that wait upon the Lord shall renew their strength; they shall mount up with wings as eagles; they shall run, and not be weary; and they shall walk and not faint. Isaiah 40:31.* He whispered a simple prayer as he looked about and lifted the binoculars for his morning survey of the countryside.

# CHAPTER 3

## RETRIBUTION

When Eli returned to the camp, the two women had prepared a meal of strip steaks, potatoes baked in the coals, and cornmeal flapjacks. Eli was surprised at the flapjacks for he had not expected the Natives to be familiar with the Southern treat. But he was more surprised when they produced some honey for them and delighted at the exceptional breakfast. He had become accustomed to nothing more than coffee, maybe a leftover biscuit, and then be on his way. As he finished his meal, he asked Wrapped in the Clouds, "Do you have a village or camp nearby?"

"We have a village, one day's ride to the north," she nodded across the road to the black-timbered mountains. The mountains were covered with pine, fir, larch, and spruce with a scattering of aspen. It was wild country, rolling hills that climbed to higher mountains, some still holding glaciers in their folds. They were in the Bitterroot Mountains, wild and rough country, and Eli had been traveling the Mullan Road, bound to the west and eventually to Walla Walla, Washington Territory. This was also the land of the Nez Perce, the Palouse, Salish, Cayuse, Coeur D'Alene and more.

Eli looked at the women, glanced to Peo Peo, and asked Wrapped in the Clouds, "Are you going to your village?"

Wrapped in the Clouds nodded, glancing to White Bird and Peo Peo.

Eli asked, "Will you be safe?"

Wrapped in the Clouds let a slow smile paint her face, and she nodded, "Yes. My son is a good hunter and warrior. It is not far, we will be safe." She paused, looked at the camp and the goods, looked back at Eli, "You have helped us, we are thankful. Do you go on?" nodding to the west and the road below their camp.

"Yes." He reached into his vest pocket and withdrew a tintype. He handed it to her, pointing to the figures in the picture, "Those are my sons. They left home and came to this country. I search for them."

Wrapped in the Clouds looked at the picture, frowned, looked at Eli and back to the picture. She leaned closer to White Bird and showed her the picture. White Bird nodded and looked at Eli as Wrapped in the Clouds responded, "We saw them."

Eli was startled, looked at the women and pointed to the picture, "You saw them? Those two men?"

"Yes. They were with a band of white men that had many long-eared pack animals with heavy loads. They were together, we have not seen two-alike before and White Bird pointed to them." Wrapped giggled as she looked at White Bird, "She sees all men, she looks for a man," she pushed at White Bird who was obviously embarrassed, and continued, "That was before we were attacked, and our men were killed."

"They were on this road?" asked Eli, pointing to the road below the camp.

"Yes," she held up her hand, four fingers extended, "this many days." She handed the tintype back to Eli, and asked, "Do you follow?"

Eli nodded, "Yes, I've been looking for them for several weeks, what you would call two moons or more, and I will follow them. I am grateful to you for telling me about them."

Eli watched as the three new friends rode from the camp to cross the gravelly bottomed St. Regis River. As they splashed across the shallow stream and mounted the far bank, Peo Peo turned back and lifted a hand high just before the three crossed the roadway and disappeared into the trees. Eli turned back to his horses, tightened the girth on the claybank. The big linebacked red dun stallion stood a good sixteen hands, but Eli was tall enough to reach over the top and fasten the tie-downs behind the cantle of his saddle. Eli stood about six foot, three inches tall, carried about two hundred fifteen pounds on his broad-shouldered frame. His dark grey wool trousers were topped with a striped white and grey linen shirt under a black leather vest. He was clean-shaven, and most women thought him to be quite handsome, although he paid little heed to the attentions of women. After graduating from West Point, his career in the army took him to Fort Laramie where he learned the ways of many Native peoples, fought some, and eventually was transferred to serve under General Sheridan in the war as a cavalry officer, leaving the army at the rank of lieutenant colonel.

Although raised in the east where his family were well-respected shipbuilders, he was more at home in the mountains of the West than among the populated cities of the East. And it was here that he searched for his wayward sons who had deserted the army just before war's end, but he only sought them to fulfill a promise to his wife to bring them home. Her untimely death was due to consumption and had snuffed the light out of their long-held dream to spend their years together on her family's farm in Kentucky, raising blooded Morgan and Tennessee Walker horses.

His thoughts of the past brought a deep sigh that lifted his shoulders as he drew deep of the clear mountain air. He finished tying down the panniers, packs, and parfleche that sat atop the packsaddle on the dapple-grey mustang gelding, grabbed up the lead rope and stepped aboard Rusty, the claybank stallion, and with a nudge of his heels, crossed the St. Regis and took to the road and the pursuit of the packtrain and his sons.

He had been traveling on the Mullan Road, a road built by the military for transporting goods from the headwaters of the Missouri River at Fort Benton, Montana Territory, to Walla Walla, Washington Territory, and the Columbia River. The search for his boys had brought him through most of Montana, Helena and Last Chance Gulch, Virginia City and Alder Gulch, and Hellgate and Bear Gulch, all recent discoveries of gold that had attracted thousands of war veterans and more, including the two young men searching for riches and a new life. He had been on the search for more than two months and it was nearing midsummer and although he had been close, he had yet to come face-to-face with his wayward sons.

The day before, the road left the Clark Fork River at the confluence with the St. Regis River, and after the night's camp and the meeting of the Nez Perce and the visit from the wolf pack, he was enjoying the quiet of the lonely mountain trail. It was beautiful but wild country and he enjoyed most everything about it. He looked about, noticing a pair of mule deer that lifted their heads from the river water to look at the passerby, heard the chatter of a squirrel high up a cottonwood that stood scolding him and his horses as their clattering hooves pounded the hard-packed trail. The flash of fur showed a long-eared jackrabbit giving a hungry coyote a workout as he ran under the long branches of a chokecherry patch and disappeared into a thicket of kinnikinnick and currant bushes.

Life was everywhere, and the beauty of the mountains seemed endless. The pungent smell of pine and spruce filled the air, and the sight of several brown-chested elk showing antlers in the velvet as they grazed the tall grasses of a park in the clearing of pines added to the beauty. But even among such beauty, Eli knew that danger and death was always as near as the next breath and when Rusty bobbed his head and snorted, ears pricked and nostrils flaring as he stutter-stepped and looked at the tree line across the river and beyond the grassy flat. A massive silver-tipped grizzly bear ambled from the trees, his rolling shoulders and swinging head told of this ruler of the woods' confidence and total lack of fear. Eli reined up and slipped the big Spencer .52-caliber rifle from the scabbard that hung on the left of the pommel of his saddle.

Eli lay the rifle across the pommel and his legs as he watched the beast go to the water. The bear, seldom making himself seen in the open and light of day, paid little attention to anything around him. He was deter-mined to get his water and bellied down on the bank, dropping his muzzle to the water and lapping up his drink with his long-curled tongue. He lifted his head to look about, paid no attention to Eli and the horses, and continued his drink. Eli knew the eyesight of the grizzly was not the best, but his sense of smell was exceptional. He felt the breeze on his face and was relieved to know the smell, strong and even repulsive though it was, of the bear came to him instead of his smell alarming the bear.

Eli sat still and the horses kept watching the bear without moving, although it was obvious they recognized the smell and were a little nervous, but they heeded the low voice of Eli as he whispered to the horses, calming them as much as possible. The big bear finished his drink, moved away from the water and took a roll in the tall grasses, came to his feet and dropped to his haunches, facing away from Eli. The grizzly began to groom himself, and slowly rose and ambled back the way he came. When he disappeared into the trees, Eli waited a short while, then nudged the horses forward, still watching the tree line, his hand gripping the Spencer.

After they passed the watering hole and a backward glance showed no sign of the beast, Eli breathed a little easier, dropped the Spencer in the scabbard, and leaned forward to stroke the neck of Rusty, "Good boy, Rusty, good boy." He pulled on the lead to bring the grey alongside and reached over and stroked the face of the grey, "You did well, boy, yessir."

It was the beginning of dusk when he neared the headwaters of the St. Regis River. What had been a free-flowing stream of crystal clear water that chuckled over the rocky bottom, was now nothing more than a giggling trickle that often disappeared into the rocks to emerge a little further downhill. But the water was clear and cold and was sufficient for the horses to get their drink and for Eli to fill his coffeepot. As he pulled the grey pack-horse near, he noticed the little mustang was favoring his left front hoof, showing a slight limp. Eli slipped to the ground, arched his back, and stretched before grabbing the reins and lead rope and taking his horses to the water. As they drank, Eli loosened the girths and stripped the gear from both. As the grey drank, Eli lifted the favored hoof and saw a stone lodged on the sole at the rear of the hoof, beside the frog. He grabbed his knife and dislodged the stone, seeing no damage, but the grey would probably be sore for a day or two.

He made camp just inside the trees above the creek bottom, where the grass was deep and the aspen clustered above the little beaver pond. He picketed the horses after they had their roll in the grass, giving them enough lead to graze and soon had a little fire going using long dead branches that would give off little or no smoke, and with it under the outspread branches of the big spruce, any smoke would dissipate before showing itself. With a meal of broiled venison, some warmed up leftover cornmeal biscuits, and a pot of hot coffee, Eli was sated and content, already looking forward to a peaceful night's sleep in the cool mountain air.

The moon was still full and bright and with a clear sky, it competed with the myriad of stars that hung in the velvety sky for the attention of the lone camper. Eli lay with hands behind his head thinking of the day before them and reckoned on resting here for a day or two, let the grey heal up and maybe get in a little meat hunting. He lay still, taking in the beauty and peacefulness of the night, smiling at the distant howl of a lonesome wolf, the nearby discordant croaking of a bullfrog, and the faraway high-pitched chirps and squeals of an osprey. He rolled to his side, mumbled a simple prayer of thanks and praise, just before dropping off to sleep.

# CHAPTER 4

## HUNT

The coffeepot rattled its lid as it perked the black brew, competing with the sizzle of the thin sliced venison steaks broiling over the open flames. Eli lifted the willow withe that held the steaks, cautiously picked one off and lay it on the last biscuit and leaned back against the rough-barked spruce to enjoy his morning meal. The golden glow of the slow rising sun showed above the timber-crested mountain that now appeared as a dark silhouette. He had looked at the grey's hoof, saw he still favored it a little, and decided to make this a day to replenish his meat supply and give the horses a rest. Although he was anxious to find the pack-train that supposedly had taken on his sons, he could not risk crippling his packhorse.

The sun had yet to crest the mountains behind him as he mounted Rusty and started up the long draw that held the headwaters of the St. Regis. The timber was thick with big spruce that had trunks bigger than he could reach around and standing well over seventy feet tall, and a scattering of fir, larch, spruce, and pine intermixed with little chance for direct sunlight to reach the floor of the forest. But an ancient trail wound through the trees, often in sight of the creek and the many beaver ponds and working its way toward the upper end of the long bowl of a valley that lay between the higher mountains. The trail and the creek made a bend to the north and back to the west to open up the valley to the morning sunlight. The trees receded and rocky shoulders pushed away from the long mountain ridge on Eli's right. The north-facing slopes on the left were thicker with timber, and when Eli saw geese dropping low, he guessed the protruding shoulder of the slope held a lake. Grazing in the bottom of the valley were several elk, the bulls with antlers in the velvet and the cows with orange calves beside. But an elk would be more meat than Eli could handle even if he smoked it all, so he continued his hunt.

The sun shone bright on the rocky slope and Eli spotted some white rumps that betrayed the presence of bighorn sheep. He grinned as he slipped the binoculars from the saddlebags, lifted the Spencer from the scabbard, and swung to the ground. He tethered Rusty in the shade with ample graze and started up the big hillside, staying just inside the tree line. Before him was the bald face of a talus slope and beyond that a long line of timber. It was beyond the timber where he saw the small herd of sheep and would use that as cover to mask his stalk.

He slowly climbed the steep hillside, stopping often to get his wind, and continuing. The altitude here was probably seven to eight thousand feet and the air was clear and thin. He paused at the crest of a shoulder, dropped to one knee and lifted the binoculars to look at

the bighorns. He breathed heavy, but still spotted the
small herd of about twenty sheep. He looked for and saw
the lead ram, a big fellow with a full curl of horn,
standing with front feet atop a big rock as he looked over
his domain. There were at least four other rams, one
almost the size of the leader, the others with horns just
over a half curl. He counted five ewes, and guessed there
were at least five, maybe more, lambs, all bouncing and
careening around, testing their mountain legs.

He replaced the binoculars in the case that hung over
one shoulder, stood, and resumed his assault on the
mountain. He had mentally mapped out his course that
would take him higher than the sheep, across the top of
the talus slope and through the line of timber. From
there, he would plan his stalk depending on where the
sheep had moved.

The sun warmed his back as he moved silently across
the rocky face above the talus, pausing often to look
around at the distant mountains of the Bitterroot Range.
They were rugged mountains, thick with timber and
rich with game, and seldom would he see a sight as
magnificent as these mountains. As he entered the trees
of the strip that separated him from the sheep, he
cautiously picked his steps, careful to keep to the
needle-carpeted game trail. As he neared the edge of the
trees, he paused, searched the far hillside and rocky-
faced slope, spotted the sheep, not far from where they
were before, but he still needed to be closer for a good
shot. He was above them, but once he stepped from the
trees, they could easily see him. If he made the slightest
sound, they would be gone before he could even lift the
Spencer for a shot. He knew they were confident of their
ability and agility to escape when in the high country
and on steep mountainsides that few predators could

climb, so they usually did not expect an attack from above.

He took another look with the binoculars, chose his route, and put the field glasses in the case. He checked the load on his Spencer and lifted his eyes to the animals. With a deep breath, he began his stalk. He moved from the trees, picking each step, watching the animals, and moving slowly but steadily. As the lead ram started to turn and move, Eli dropped to his uphill knee and froze, leaning into the hillside, making as small an image as possible. The big ram moved to another promontory, looked around and back at the herd, and dropped his head for a mouthful of lichen. Eli moved, wanting to get to his chosen spot quickly, but silently. Just another fifteen yards, to a clump of oak brush, and he moved, watching the animals and each step.

He dropped to one knee beside the brush, looked over the edge to see the animals beginning to move, felt the breeze on his face and frowned as he looked about, wondering if they picked up the scent of another predator. He could wait no longer. Lifting the Spencer to his shoulder, he began to sight on the big ram, but the leader was pushed off his promontory by the other ram that had almost a full curl. The rams often had jousting battles, and it appeared that is what the younger one had in mind.

The lead ram turned, tossed his head, and lowered the horns as he pawed at the ground before him. The younger ram did the same and as if on some silent cue, both rose up on hind legs and lunged forward, crashing their horns together in a sound that bounced off the walls of the mountains and echoed down the valley. The brutes stood, shaking their heads and circled one another, until the younger rose up again, prompting the bigger ram to do the same and they charged again, slamming into one another with a resounding crash that echoed again and again. Eli watched as the two combatants continued their sparring, but he looked at the rest of the herd as they stood watching the two bighorn gladiators. As the fight slowed, Eli picked one of the younger rams, made his sight, cocked the hammer, and pulled the trigger. The Spencer bucked and roared, the sound echoing as the bullet sped on its way and slammed into the lower chest of the ram, knocking him to the ground to tumble further down the slope. The herd jumped as if joined together and bounded away to disappear into the upper reaches of the basin where the trees hid their escape.

Eli came to his feet, looking about, and started down the slope to his quarry. The ram had come to a stop on the crest of a rocky escarpment and Eli dropped beside it to begin dressing out the animal. He made short work of field-dressing and with the Spencer slung over one shoulder, he grabbed the horns and began pulling the carcass behind him. But steep hillside made the carcass tumble downhill quickly and tripped Eli, making him fall to the ground, catching himself on the heels of his outstretched hands and scraping them on the rough limestone rocks. He banged a knee, fell to one shoulder, and dropped to his haunches as he caught his footing to keep from sliding the rest of the way. He sat, shaking his head and chuckling at himself at getting taken down by a dead sheep.

He brushed himself off, got another hold, and dragged the carcass the rest of the way to the bottom, and on to the trees where Rusty was tethered. With the ram over the horse's haunches, Eli took to the game trail and returned to his camp, only to find he had company in the form of striped-back hissing badger that glared at what he thought was an intruder. The badger had been digging at the edge of the camp where Eli had buried the scraps and trimmings from his breakfast steaks, and he was not happy with the presence of the big horse and rider. Eli slid to the ground, Winchester in hand and talking to Rusty to keep him calm but the big horse liked the visitor even less than the badger liked getting interrupted. As Rusty backed away, Eli watched the badger, knowing they were worthy adversaries, and jacked a round in the chamber of the Winchester. He did not want to kill the animal, but he was not going to let him stay in the camp.

Eli stomped his feet and shouted, trying to get the big rodent to leave, but the badger was afraid of nothing, and he hissed and snarled at Eli. Eli hollered again, lifting the Winchester to his shoulder, and when the badger charged, he had to shoot. The rifle barked and the bullet hit the ground under the badger's chin but did not slow his charge. Eli jacked another round, stepping back, but felt a rock behind him, stumbled and fell to his back. Wide-eyed, he rolled to the side, searching for the badger and seeing it still coming, he snapped off another shot almost point-blank. The bullet tore into the rodent's chest and stopped him, dropping him to the ground as if he had been poleaxed. Eli scrambled to his feet, jacking another round into the chamber as he watched the smelly badger, then poked it with the muzzle. When it did not respond, Eli breathed a sigh of relief and slowly walked back to retrieve Rusty and his bounty.

Rusty stepped wide of the badger, looking at it all the while, and was visibly relieved when Eli picketed him alongside the grey and well away from the carcass of the rodent. Eli chuckled, grabbed his shovel and began to dig a pit to bury the smelly fur-bearing stinker. Once that was done, he set about butchering the sheep. He planned on smoking most of the meat, but not till after dark, in the meantime, he would finish the task of butchering and fix himself a little supper.

# CHAPTER 5

## BITTERROOTS

The long shadows of the early morning stretched across the Sohon Pass as Eli took to the road over the saddle and dropped downhill to the valley of the Coeur d'Alene River. The Mullan Road would follow this river as it twisted and turned through the thickly timbered mountains that lay in the shadow of the Bitterroot Range. With an additional two days behind him, the road forked, with the original route turning to the southwest. Eli had heard of the two roads, the original going south of Lake Coeur d'Alene, the other going around the north of the lake. But he also knew the southern route would be shorter and since he was not traveling with a wagon, he opted for the shorter route that would take him over the Bitterroot Range and the Saint Joe River.

———

ELI SAT on the south bank of the Saint Joe River watching the line in the water as he was hoping to catch some fish for supper. Rusty and the grey grazed beside him, the gear stacked under a big cottonwood near the riverbank. Eli was leaning back against a big rock, his hat tipped over his eyes as the sun lay lazily on the western horizon and bounced the last of its rays off the rippling water. Eli looked at Rusty, "You know boy, I don't know about you, but for a while there I thought you were gonna grow scales an' I was gonna start croakin' like a bullfrog! We crossed the St. Regis and the Coeur d'Alene Rivers so many times I thought we'd never dry off! But for right now, we're warm, dry, and hungry, so if you'll be so kind as to stay away from the water maybe one o' them big hungry trout will volunteer for my supper. After all, you're gettin' yore fill o' that nice grass there, so I'm thinkin' it's my turn."

The tug on the line brought his attention back to his fishing and he sat up, lifting the pole and reeling in the line. After a short fight, he finally landed the big rainbow on the grass in front of the stallion and quickly grabbed it to give the coup de grâce and begin his preparation for supper. As he unhooked his prize, he was startled by a voice from the trees, "Catch another'n, I'm hungry, too!"

Eli frowned, dropping the fish at his feet and surreptitiously lowered his hand to the butt of his Colt as he turned to face the voice. He was surprised to see a woman, a little ruffled and dirty, hair askew, but she pushed the hair back, showing a pleasant face with bright blue eyes, dimpled cheeks, and a broad smile.

"Whatsamatta, ain't you ever seen a woman before?" she laughed as she stepped from the trees, leading a lone horse behind her.

"Well, I can't rightly say I've ever seen a woman alone in this kind of wilderness before."

She came a little closer, dropped her eyes to a big rock

and took a seat, dropping the reins of her horse and letting her graze. Both Eli and Rusty noticed the good-looking palomino mare that tossed her head as she casually walked to water's edge, glancing back at the stallion. The horse appeared to be in better shape than the woman, but both showed their quality and told of better days. The woman looked at Eli, "I'm Donna Kennedy, and like I said, I'm hungry!" She took a deep breath and relaxed on the rock, looking at Eli.

Eli looked at her, down at the trout, and began re-baiting the hook before casting the line out again. Once the bait sunk, he turned to look back at his visitor, "I'm Elijah, Elijah McCain." He nodded to the line, "We should have another'n soon." He nodded to the trees, "My gear's over there if you're up to gettin' the coffeepot and skillet so we can cook 'em, unless you want yours baked in the coals."

"Howdy Elijah, pleased to meet'chu," she responded, rising and starting to the packs. She dug through the panniers, found the pot and pan, a bag of cornmeal, the Dutch oven, and some pork belly. With arms full she returned to the rock, looked around and began gathering firewood. She glanced to Eli, "Caught'ny yet?"

"Five or six, but threw 'em back. They's too little for a hungry woman like you."

"I ain't partic'lar, just hungry."

"When's the last time you ate?"

"Couple days ago."

Curiosity was tugging at his mind, but he chose to let her tell her story in her time. It was not his way to be overly inquisitive with strangers, especially women. A tug on the line brought his attention back to the water and he quickly landed another nice trout but thought it best to try for another one since he had an especially hungry visitor. He propped the pole between some rocks and set about cleaning the two trout, both about the same size—just a little over fifteen inches each. He had no sooner finished cleaning the second than his pole bobbed, and he jumped to catch it before it disappeared into the water. Another, even larger, trout had taken the bait and now lay beside the others.

Eli walked back to the beginnings of the fire, saw Donna on her knees fanning the little flames, and said, "Don't take what I'm about to say wrong, but there's an extra shirt in my bedroll, and some lye soap in the saddlebags, if you're of a mind. I'll be glad to tend to things here."

She rocked back on her heels, and grinned, "Are you saying I could use a bath?"

Eli chuckled, "No, ma'am, wouldn't presume such a thing. It's just the few women I've known place considerable importance on fixin' up for supper, so I just thought," he paused, trying to backtrack, "but if'n you don't want to, why..." he shrugged.

"It sounds wonderful. Did you see a good place?"

Eli grinned, nodding upstream, "I'm guessin' there might be a backwater pool the other side of that bend beyond o' those bushes yonder."

She rose to her feet, "I already found the soap, and I'll wash out this shirt," she said as she pinched a piece of the material at her side, "but it'd be nice to have a clean one on."

"Take your time, we ain't goin' nowhere," chuckled Eli, sitting on the rock beside the fish and reaching for the cornmeal.

———

ELI TOOK his time as he prepared the meal, starting with making cornmeal biscuits in the Dutch oven. Once they were prepared, he dragged some hot coals from the fire to the side, placed the Dutch oven on the coals, more on the lid, and started with the fish. He fried some of the excess fat from the pork-belly, rolled the fish in the extra cornmeal and put two in the pan to begin frying, setting the third one to the side. With some onions in the fat with the fish, the aroma was stout, but pleasant. The coffeepot began to dance as the trout sizzled and Eli pulled the pot back, dropped a handful of grounds into the water, and replaced the pot.

With the fish and onions on a tin plate, the coffeepot settled to the side, Eli scraped the coals off the top of the Dutch oven and pulled it away from the fire. He sat back, glanced to the stream and saw the woman coming from the bushes, a blanket and clothes under one arm and a smile splitting her face as she called out, "Dinner ready?"

Eli chuckled, and answered, "Yes dear!"

Donna giggled, walked closer and smiled, "Dear is it?"

"Well you're already treating me like a wife would, so…" Eli shrugged, grinning at his visitor.

As she seated herself on the big rock, she looked at the offering, "Mmmmm, looks good! And I'm famished. Let's eat!"

"Uh, don't you think we oughta say a short prayer of thanks, first?" asked Eli, removing his hat and bowing his head.

"Oh, yeah," mumbled Donna, bowing her head.

Eli smiled and began, "Dear Lord, we are thankful…" and continued with his prayer of thanksgiving and asking for guidance and safety, and finished with an "Amen," which was echoed by Donna as she reached for a plate.

She finished her fish and onions, three biscuits, two cups of coffee, and sat staring at the big fish in the frying pan, waiting anxiously for more. Eli chuckled as he looked at her, "It'll be ready soon enough. Staring won't hurry it up."

Donna laughed, shook her head, relaxed, and sat back a bit as she looked at Eli. "Aren't you gonna ask?"

Eli frowned, "Ask what?"

"What I'm doin' out here!"

"I thought you'd tell me if and when you wanted."

"I will, after I have some more fish!" she laughed, shaking her head again and watching as Eli lifted the big trout from the pan, to put it on her plate. She grinned, tearing into the soft meat, careful of the fine bones, but hesitating not a bit. Eli looked at her, the dark hair and deep blue eyes that spoke of mystery and mischief, she had a figure that caught the eye of most men and the envy of women, and she carried herself with a natural confidence, matching the pace of any man, stride for stride, yet all the while never losing a bit of her womanliness. She finished the last of the fish, looked at Eli as she licked her fingers, and said, "I'm sorry, I didn't save any for you!"

Eli grinned, "I'm fine, thank you."

She set her tin pan plate aside, reached for the coffeepot, sat back and looking at Eli, began, "We, my husband and I, were coming from WallaWalla, headed for the goldfields in Montana Territory." She breathed deep, remembering, trying to maintain her composure, "My husband, Hank, was a good-looking devil but he wasn't much for working. He thought we could go to the goldfields, get rich, and live happily ever after. He wasn't much good in the mountains either, that's how we got into trouble. He had heard about the lower route of the

Mullan Road and thought we'd save time, so we started west through the mountains. It was the beginning of the third day in the mountains that we came to a rockslide that covered the trail. I suggested we go down to the bottom and work our way around, but he was determined to cross it, and started out across the slide-rock."

She shook her head and looked at the ground, breathing deep, then lifted her eyes to Eli, "He told me to wait, he'd try first. He was leading the packhorse, jerking him is more like it, and he was about halfway across when his horse dropped a leg into a hole, stumbled to the side, broke his leg and threw Hank. He pulled on the lead of the packhorse as he tumbled, jerked the packhorse off balance and he fell, two legs broke, and when Hank finally stopped, he had split his head wide open and spilled out what few brains he had," she paused, snarled, "stupid fool!"

"So, I had to shoot the horses, tried to drag him off the slide, but had to bury him under the rocks," she dropped her head, her anger and sorrow fighting as she dabbed her eyes, took another breath. "I went below the slide and around, then had to walk back to try to get what few supplies I could and kept comin'. Why? I dunno!" She grabbed a twig and tossed it aside in anger and frustration.

"How long ago was that?" asked Eli, speaking softly.

Donna looked up at him, "Two, three days, I think. Not sure."

"So, what'chu gonna do now?" asked Eli.

Donna looked at him, shook her head and looked down at the river below them, back to Eli, "Never really thought about it. We came from WallaWalla. Didn't have much there, sold out and took what we had to head west. Now…" she shrugged, letting a few tears make trails down her cheeks. She dabbed at them, stifled a sob, and looked at Eli, "Any ideas?"

Eli grinned, "Well, I'm going *to* WallaWalla, and further probably. You're welcome to ride with me. Maybe we can come up with an idea or two while we ride."

She sighed, shook her head, chuckled, "Guess it doesn't make much difference now."

# CHAPTER 6

## CLEARWATER

"If Hank knew what he was talkin' about, those are the Clearwater Mountains," stated Donna, nodding to the mountains before them.

"They look to be just as rugged as the Bitterroots," responded Eli, looking about. They were following the original route of the Mullan Road, even though this route had few travelers, none with wagons, and those they did meet were anxiously headed for the goldfields and took no time to stop and visit. They passed the site of the rockslide that had become the stone mausoleum for her husband and spotted some carrion eating varmints fighting over the remains of the two horses, even though Donna had tried to push some rocks down on them. There was no evidence that her husband's internment had been bothered. With the rockslide behind them, Donna became more talkative and the riding more pleasant as they became more acquainted with one another.

"That's what Hank called the St. Maries River," declared Donna, pointing to the stream below. They were still back in the trees when she spotted the silvery ribbon winding through the edge of the flats. The road builders had kept to the flats and the rolling hills as much as possible and usually followed the route of a creek or river or previous trail used by the Natives. Now the trail they followed came from the higher mountains, kept to the rolling timbered hills, and dropped into the valley of the St. Maries River.

Eli glanced to the sky, the sun was lowering near the mountains and Eli guessed there would be about another half hour before the onset of dusk and pointed to a grassy clearing on the far side of the river, "Let's make camp there."

"Suits me. I'll follow you across the river," answered Donna, nodding to the rippling waters.

Eli glanced to some rimrock-shouldered hills to his right, ahead to the little river with scattered cotton-woods, alders, and willows and started to a break in the brush and a rocky shoal at river's edge. He let Rusty drop his head to the water, watched the grey do the same and when heads came up for a look around, Eli nudged the big stallion into the water. The river was no more that seventy feet wide and about knee deep on the stallion and the crossing was easily made with the palomino mare bringing up the rear.

Donna called out, "We havin' fish for supper again?"

"No, I think we'll have lamb chops!"

"Where you gonna get lamb chops?" asked a bewildered Donna as they pushed into the chosen clearing for their camp.

"You'll see, you'll see," chuckled Eli, grinning at his new traveling companion.

"How 'bout some lamb chops for us!" came a growling voice from the trees. Eli dropped his hand to the Colt in his holster as he turned, but the voice barked, "Don't do it pilgrim, less'n you wanna die!"

As Eli slowly turned in his saddle, he saw three mounted men push from the trees, all holding pistols aimed toward the two that sat their saddles as the horses shook the water free from their crossing. But Rusty was skittish at the movements and turned his head to face the others, sidestepping as he did, causing Eli to be facing the visitors. Donna reined her mount around to side Eli while the grey, also a touch skittish, sidestepped and turned on the far side of Rusty. The three men, one wearing a butternut-and-grey Kepi hat, the others wearing dark, floppy felt hats. All were roughly attired, unkempt, and slovenly. The speaker was the biggest and nearest of the three, leaned forward, elbows on the pommel of his saddle and grinned to show tobacco-stained teeth, several missing, as he sneered at Donna, "Well now, what have we here! If it ain't a woman, and not too bad lookin' one, neither!"

"Hehehehe," cackled the cap wearing skinny one who sat in the middle, waving his Remington Army pistol around carelessly as he cackled.

"Can I have her first, Lige?" asked the third man as he nudged his mount forward, glaring at Donna.

"You know better'n to ask that, Winnie!" snarled Lige, snarling at the third man who was panting like a dog.

Donna lifted her left hand to her forehead and feigned fright and in a high-pitched squeal, "Oh lawdy, what am I to do!" she wailed, winking at Eli.

"I can hep ya!" called Winnie, glancing to the skinny one beside him, "You stay back Bones!" Winnie turned to face Donna and started to nudge his mount forward just as Donna brought a pistol from her back and blasted the scoundrel. The bullet took him on the chin, driving through the bone and into the man's throat that spouted blood and tobacco juice as he tumbled backward. The shot spooked his horse as did the kick from his rider and the horse dropped his head between his feet, bent in the middle, kicked at the stars, jumped into the water and splashed across the little river.

The blast from the pistol shot by Donna prompted Eli to dig heels into Rusty's sides and drive toward the other two. Rusty drove into the horse of Lige, driving him back on his heels, causing Lige to grab at the saddle horn just as Rusty and Eli crashed by with Eli smashing the barrel of his pistol to the back of Lige's head, knocking him from the saddle of the staggering horse. He fell to the ground, only to be trampled by his own horse as it fought for footing on the slick grass. Eli urged Rusty to continue his charge, but the skinny runt was lifting his pistol to fire just as Eli dropped the hammer on his Colt, the bullet taking the skinny one high in the chest, smashing his sternum and driving through to shatter the bones in his spine.

As Rusty lunged past, the skinny one fell limply from his saddle and the bay horse, rib bones and hip bones showing, staggered to the side, but kept his feet under him. Eli whirled Rusty around to face the pandemonium, only to see the sorrel of Lige standing head down, shaking, but looking at the remains of his rider. Across the creek, Winnie's bay was lazily grazing on the grass. Eli looked at the downed men, the trampled body of the ringleader, the lecherous Winnie lay on his back, sightless eyes staring at the clouds and the bottom of his face and neck nothing but bloody pulp. The skinny one lay crumpled on his side, unmoving, one leg twisted under him. The sudden thunder of the pandemonium had stilled and the moan of the wind through the trees blended gently with the chuckling river as it washed over the rocks.

Eli looked at Donna who sat still in her saddle, leaning forward on her pommel with the pistol still in her hand as she stared at the bodies before her. She lifted her eyes to Eli, "I never shot a man before. Wanted to, but never did," she paused, looking at Eli with pleading eyes, "I don't want to ever do that again."

Eli looked at the woman who appeared forlorn, "Let's move upstream a mite, find another camp. I'll come back and tend to this mess."

She nodded and sat up, nudged her palomino toward Eli, and followed as he led the grey packhorse and pushed through the trees to search for another campsite well away from the stench of death. The long branches of spruce seemed to reach out and try to sweep them off their saddles, the bushy headed ponderosa waved high overhead, yielding to the early evening breeze, and the early arriving turkey buzzards had begun their tireless circling overhead, anticipating their evening meal.

The clearing opened before them, grass stretching to the riverbank and tucking itself under the overhanging willows, the lowering sun offering ample light to set up camp as Donna pushed her palomino alongside Eli, "Looks alright to me. We can tether the horses yonder," pointing to a cluster of aspen waving their leaves as an invitation, "and I'll start our fire there!" pointing to the tall ponderosa that shaded the south edge of the camp.

"I'll picket the horses and strip the packs from the grey, then I'll go back and take care of that," stated Eli, nodding in the direction of the previous camp.

Donna stepped down, handed Eli the reins to her palomino, and began searching for firewood. Eli picketed the grey and the palomino, stripped the gear from the grey, and grabbed the small shovel and stepped back aboard his claybank. He nudged his mount near the girl who was down on one knee, starting the fire. "The meat is in the pannier, cut it as you will. There's also some cornmeal and such."

"I'll find it."

"Keep a watch, those might not be the only ones riding this trail. Can't be too careful."

She turned to look up at him, put her hand on the grip of her pistol that was holstered at her back, smiled, "I'll be alright."

Eli grinned, nodded, and started for the previous camp. When he returned, he was leading two of the horses from the attackers. Donna rose, shaded her eyes from the setting sun and asked, "I thought there were three?"

"The boney one had a broke leg, had to put him down. Don't rightly know what we'll do with these two, but…" he shrugged as he stepped down. He picketed the horses and returned to the fire and a smiling Donna as she stood proprietarily before the cookfire.

"It smells good. Ready?"

"It is, thank you." She waved to a log and said, "Be seated, sir, and I'll serve your dinner."

Eli chuckled, glanced at the woman as she dished up his plate, "Sounds mighty fancy for the woods."

As she handed him the plate, she explained, "The meat is from the pannier and I don't know what it is, but I'm thinking it was some kind of sheep. The vegetables are onions and cattail shoots, the biscuits are fresh baked in the Dutch oven, and the gravy is a surprise. And, I have a special dessert when you're finished, sir." She curtsied, backed away, and began to fill her own plate.

Eli grinned, "Why, thank you, ma'am, that's mighty fine of you," and added, "May we give thanks for this fine meal?"

"Certainly, sir," she answered, smiling and bowing her head.

Eli said the short prayer of thanksgiving, finished with an "Amen," and heard a soft answer from the woman.

It took no more than the first bite to tell him this was a fine meal, and he lifted his eyes to the woman, "This is quite good. With cookin' like this, I reckon your husband musta packed on the pounds!"

"Well, to be honest, he wasn't really my husband. Never had one, but he was the closest thing to one and he did more drinking than eating." She paused, reached for the coffeepot to refill their cups, "Always wanted a home, family, and more. But...the pickin's are slim up here. Most of the men are more interested in gold than family. I came up from the coast on a riverboat, spent my last money on the ticket, and met Hank on the boat. He was a gambler and a drinker, but he offered to help get me set up in the goldfield, so..." She shrugged.

"Set up?" asked Eli, finishing his food and lifting his cup for a sip of black brew.

"Ummhmm. I'm a singer and can usually get on at a tavern or some such. I've heard some of these gold towns even put in theaters. I had my trousseau but when the packhorse went down, I thought I was doin' good gettin' some foodstuffs." She looked up at Eli, gave her eyes a bit of a squint as she glared at him, "And before you start passin' judgment, mister, I'll have you know I have never been 'one of the girls' and never 'entertained' any men!"

Eli leaned back, holding up one hand, "Now, wait just a minute! I would not presume to pass judgment on anyone, much less someone that can shoot like you!" he grinned as he chuckled.

Donna leaned back and let a slow smile paint her face. "So, you like your dinner?"

"Yes, ma'am."

"And you're not just saying that because I can shoot straight?"

"Would it be safe to answer otherwise?" chuckled Eli.

"No, and don't you forget it. Now, how 'bout some dessert?" she asked as she reached for a pan full of berries. She stretched out to Eli, offering him the pan, and he scooped some onto his plate. He recognized black currants, gooseberries, and mooseberries. He smiled up at her and slid some onto his fork and began to enjoy the rare treat. Donna smiled and did the same, looked up at Eli, "So, now it's your turn to tell me about yourself!"

# Chapter 7

# Company

With the Clearwater Mountains at their back, the distant peaks with their heads in the clouds, Eli and Donna looked westward as the trail rode the shoulder of the rolling and timbered hills. A big flat-top mesa with rimrock near the crest, stretched out to the north as it sided a shallow creek that they would soon be following to the west. The trail was easy-going and wide enough for the two to ride side by side and at Donna's urging, Eli shared his story.

"So, after my wife passed, I set out to fulfill my covenant with her and find the boys. After chasin' 'em through the different goldfields, Last Chance Gulch, Alder Gulch, Bear Gulch, and a few places in between, the last word I had about 'em was they were headed this way with a packtrain." Eli shrugged, lifted his eyes to the surrounding country.

"You've had quite a life!" responded Donna, glancing sidelong at her traveling companion.

"Oh, I s'pose, but each in his or her own way has quite a life, don't they?" asked Eli.

"I reckon. It just seems the other person's life is always more exciting than your own."

Eli frowned, cocked his head to the side to look at Donna, "Hmmm, unless I miss my guess, I reckon I've probably lived about ten or more years than you have, so you have a lot of living to catch up to me, and if the last few days are any sample, I think you've quite a bit of excitement waiting to be lived."

Donna smiled, looked around, and began to sing softly.

> There's a wideness in God's mercy, like the wide-
>     ness of the sea;
> There's a kindness in God's justice, which is more
>     than liberty.
> There is welcome for the sinner, and more graces
>     for the good;
> There is mercy with the Savior, there is healing in
>     His blood.
> If our love were but more simple, we should rest
>     upon God's word,
> And our lives would be illumined by the presence
>     of our Lord.

She continued to hum the tune, glanced at Eli, "Have you heard that one before?"

Eli dropped his eyes, "I had a colored sergeant that had a deep bass voice and near the end of the war, he sang that, of course not as light and pretty as you, but if I remember right, there were several other verses."

"Yes, but I can't remember them all. It's a beautiful song and I learned it at home. It was a new song that our church pianist brought in for our choir. But I haven't heard it much since."

The road crossed a little willow-lined creek that came from the northwest and the horses dropped their noses in the crystal clear water for a quick drink before stepping across the shallow stream. A glance off his left shoulder revealed a grassy flat and cottonwoods at the creek bank of the larger stream that had sided the trail all morning. Eli nodded, "Let's do our noonin' yonder," as he reined the big stallion toward the shade of the trees.

They made short work of the leftover biscuits and strips of broiled meat for their noon meal, washed it down with coffee and at Eli's suggestion, they stretched out in the shade to give the horses a break. But a lance of sun through the cottonwoods brought Eli awake just as Rusty nuzzled his cheek and turned to look back to the roadway to see two mounted riders, both leading pack mules, headed east on the Mullan Road. Eli sat up, drew up his knees and wrapped his arms around them, and pushed his hat back on his head as he watched the two travelers pass. Eli knew their horses were hidden in the shadows of the big trees and the nearby willows, but he was not anxious to meet up with anyone, not after the last run-in. A whisper came from nearby when Donna said, "They must be headin' to the goldfields."

"Ummhmm. Glad we were off the road when they passed. I'm not feelin' too friendly since our last set-to."

"Neither am I, but we'll probably meet others."

"Ummhmm, so we might as well get back on the road, make some time while we can."

The trail followed the same creek for several more miles until the road crossed over what appeared to be near the headwaters of the creek, and sidled up the face of the opposite hill and broke over a saddle crossing and dropped into a long, wide valley that stretched out westward. The road followed a long ridge before bending around the nose of the ridge and pointing directly west. Donna pointed to the creek in the bottom, "Hank said that was called Hangman Creek. He said he heard a fella talkin' 'bout it and it got its name a few years back when the soldiers caught up with a war party of about seventeen Palouse Indians and hung 'em."

Eli frowned. "What for?"

Donna chuckled. "Hank said there had been a war on an' the soldiers chased 'em down. Other'n that, I dunno."

The timbered hills shouldered back, and a wide, flat valley stretched before them. Eli reined up, leaned on the pommel and took a deep breath, "You know, I love the mountains, the high-country air, and all that, but after that stretch, it sure looks good to see the wide-open spaces."

Donna looked at the wide vista, back to Eli, "If I remember right, just up there a ways is where the other road of the Mullan joins this one."

Eli glanced to the lowering sun, "Then maybe we'll find us a campsite soon. There will probably be more travelers from the upper road or going that way. Either way, it's gettin' late 'nuff for stoppin'."

The road continued to side the little creek as it wound through the thicker pines that dropped off a tall shoulder of the hills to the south. The lower hill on the north side pushed back from the creek, appearing to be crowded out by the willows and alders that grew thick in the bottom, but the road pushed through and once again broke into the open. From the slight rise of the road, they could see into the flats and at the edge of the trees just below them, Eli saw the dingy white bonnets of several wagons. He nodded that direction, "Looks like a bunch of wagons, probably headed to the goldfields like the rest. Let's cross over the creek, make our camp on the far side there, back up against those tall ponderosa."

"Suits me, I'm gettin' hungry anyway," answered Donna, grinning at Eli.

Eli shook his head, chuckling, "Aren't you always?"

"Hmm, no. Just lately. Must be the comp'ny," she laughed as they nudged their mounts toward the creek.

As they started to cross, Eli glanced to the side to see the back of a head showing above the willows and the wearer working a fishing pole, apparently landing a big fish. The man scrambled, twisted, groaned and mumbled, oblivious to any company, and when he succeeded in landing the fish, "Finally!" he declared as he bent to unhook his prize.

Eli called out as the horses waded the creek, "Don't catch 'em all, we might want some."

The fisherman, surprised, jumped up and looked at the two horsemen, frowned, and called out, "Colonel? Colonel McCain?"

Eli reined up and twisted around in his saddle and looked at the fisherman. Standing before him was a mountain of a colored man, bib overalls and a homespun shirt that was rolled up to show massive forearms, but the wide grin on the man's face dispelled any reason for concern when he pushed back his hat, and said, "I declare! It really is you!" and a deep rumbling laugh shook the man's sizable belly. "It's me, Sergeant Major Moses Carpenter!"

Eli's face split in a smile as he slid from his saddle and splashed into the creek to meet his longtime friend as the two big men wrapped one another in a bear hug that was bathed in laughter and back slaps. When the two pushed apart to look at one another, Eli asked,

"What are you doin' up here in the middle of nowhere —fishing?"

"I'se hungry! And muh family's hungry! And I has me a appetite fo' fish! An' I caught me some too!" he chuckled as he waved his hand back to the fish that lay in the grass, lined out by size. "How's 'bout you an' yo' missus joinin' us?"

Eli chuckled, "Ah, she's not my missus, but she is a good friend. And we'd be delighted!" He looked about, "We're gonna make camp yonder by the big trees, an' we'll put the horses up and be back to join you. Can we bring anything?"

The big man grinned, "Coffee?"

"We can do it. You with the wagons yonder?"

"That's us. We gots five wagons an' families, too. You'll be almighty welcome, Colonel."

"War's over. It's Eli."

"Yassuh, an' I be Moses, suh."

Eli grinned, slapped his friend on the shoulder and turned back to his horse and Donna.

## CHAPTER 8

## FREIGHTERS

"He was kind of a big brother to me growing up. He worked at the family's shipyards, watched out for me when I was trying to learn the different jobs, always friendly and protective," mused Eli as they stepped down from the horses and began making camp.

"Is he the one that sang that song you spoke of earlier?"

"He's the one. He had enlisted at the beginning of the war, worked his way up through the ranks, but we were never together until towards the end. He was my sergeant major in my last command at Appomattox." Eli grew thoughtful as he stripped the gear from the horses and picketed them. It was more of a task now with the two horses from the outlaws, but it was quickly done. When the bedrolls were laid out, the cookfire readied, gear stashed, Eli looked to Donna, "You ready?"

She smiled, "Yessir, Colonel, sir," and gave a mock salute.

Eli chuckled, "You might'a made a soldier, but..." he shrugged as they started toward the camp of the wagons.

————

"COLONEL, uh, Eli, this is muh wife, Ethel, an' muh son, Lucas," stated Moses, proudly standing beside his lady and son.

"Pleased to meet you, ma'am, Lucas," nodded Eli, tipping his hat to the woman and extending his hand to shake with Lucas. "And this is my friend, Donna Kennedy," he explained, nodding to her.

The introductions continued as they walked from wagon to wagon, first it was his close friend, Johnathan Green, his wife, Mildred, and daughter Hannah. "We served together in the Fifth Cavalry 'fore I was transferred to your unit," explained Moses.

Down the line came the rest, beginning with William Harrison from the Forty-First Infantry and his wife, Abigail, and daughter Leah. Then Matthew McCoslin from the Twenty-Nineth Infantry, and his wife, Rebecca, and sons, Benjamin and Ethan. The last wagon was the Conklin family, Ezra served in the 116th Infantry and his wife, Anna, and son Gideon.

As they walked together back to Moses' wagon, Eli asked, "So, all the men served with the Union?"

"Yessuh, an' we had two other families. One family, the Cantons, dropped out in Nebraska Territory. He had a son that mustered out and had already got him a farm started and asked his Pappy to stay, so they did. Then we had a couple, the Whitcombs, they was at the tail end an' when we was attacked by some Injuns, he was kilt an' we couldn't get her to leave his grave." He shook his head in remembrance, tears welling up in his eyes that he dabbed away. "But you two jus' sit yo'sefs down right thar," motioning to a bench alongside the makeshift table, "an' we'll us have some supper!"

As they dined they talked, and Eli asked, "So, where are you bound for now?"

"Oh, same place we stah'ted fo', Washington Territ'ry. We wants to git as fah away from them fo'ks in the South, and they ways, as we can! An' the fah side of them mountains," nodding to the west, "is as fah as we can go!" He chuckled as he looked back at Eli, showing a wide grin. "And how come is it we run into you, Colonel?"

Eli shook his head at his friend's continued use of his rank, but said nothing more about it, as he began to explain about his search for his boys who had deserted and gone west. He looked to Moses, "But, if you folks came across Nebraska Territory, how did you get this far north, the Oregon Trail is south of here?"

"When we heard 'bout the gold strike, we thot we'd give it a try, so at Fo't Lah'mie, we took off on the Bozeman way, but when we got into them goldfields, we wasn't made too welcome. We decided that since we don't know nuthin' 'bout gold nohow, we'd just keep goin' to Washington Terri'try, so, he'h we is!" he laughed, his belly bouncing as he folded his hands across his bib overalls.

"How are you fixed for supplies, ammunition, and such?" asked Eli.

"Wal, we doin' aw'right. Could use mo' but some o' dem sto's don' wanna sell to us'ns." He shook his head, "That's why we's thankful fo' the coffee," he chuckled, making light of the challenges.

———

AFTER SWAPPING a few more tales and memories, Eli and Donna rose to return to their camp. "Uh, fo' you go, I was thinkin', after what you said 'bout those fellas what attacked you, that mebbe it'd be better fo' all of us, if'n you was to travel wit' us? What say?" asked Moses, looking somberly at Eli with a glance to Donna.

Eli let a slow grin spread, and nodded, "You might be right about that, Moses. But if you think you're gonna drink all my coffee, you might wanna whoa up with that kinda thinkin'," chuckled Eli, stretching out his hand to shake with his friend.

"See, there ya' go, thinkin' the wust o' me already!" laughed the big man, clasping Eli's hand in both of his and shaking heartily.

"First light then?" asked Eli.

"Yassuh, fust light!" replied Moses.

————

THE ROAD TOOK them south toward the long line of timber-covered rolling hills that stretched across the horizon before them. As they got into the timbered hills, the first few miles were a steady climb and the horses leaned into their traces to pull the wagons up the grade. As they crested the climb, the road bent more to the south and was easygoing as it snaked through the hills. Moses pointed to the bald face of a hill on his right, "Now see there, tha's sumpin' I just don' unnerstan', how so many these mountains is bald on one side like a baby's bottom, and hairy with timbeh on t'other. How come is that, Colonel, suh?" Moses was riding one of the horses Eli had taken from the outlaws, complete with saddle, rifle, and the belt with holster and pistol. Eli had given the other horse to Moses' boy who was more of a man than a boy.

"I don't rightly know, Moses, but I've seen that throughout the Rockies. It's the south-facing slopes that are usually bald, maybe it's because of the hot early sun, and the north slopes that enjoy the later-day sunshine without the blazing heat and those slopes are thick with trees."

"The Lawd sho do things diff'nt wherever He may be," declared the big man, shaking his head and smiling. "But it sho' nuff almighty purty!"

"It is that, Moses, it is that."

The road bent around the point of a shoulder of a long ridge and the land opened its arms wide to show the beginnings of a long valley and wide-open spaces beyond, but the road before them was lifting a cloud of dust as a line of freighters came around a wide curve and lined out before them. There were seven or eight freighters, each pulled by a team of no less than six oxen. Bullwhackers were walking alongside the lead pair of oxen, using a whip and a lash to add force to their shouted commands, keeping the big beasts moving, as their heads swayed side to side with their steps, plodding onward.

Eli motioned to a stretch of grass between the road and a small creek, "Let's pull off there, give 'em room to pass. And we can take our noonin' there where there's plenty of fresh water."

"Sounds good to me!" answered Moses as he stood in his stirrups and turned back to face the wagons, motioning them to pull off the road when they came to this point. The last of the wagons pulled up behind the others, just as the freighters and their ox teams came near. The bullwhackers scowled at the families, but continued with their incessant chatter, cursing, and coaxing of the bovines, giving little heed to the women and children of the wagons.

Eli and Donna had stepped down and led their animals to the water before the freighters neared, and now led the horses to stand between the wagons and the road, looking at the freighters as they passed. Eli nodded to the men, saying nothing, but he heard several of the bullwhackers voice their dislike of the coloreds coming into this part of the country. One burly, scruffy-looking man with a flat-topped sailor's tarred hat cocked at a jaunty angle, shouted, "You don' belong hyar, go back where ya' come from!"

Eli spoke up, "And where'd you come from, sailor boy?"

The burly man stopped, letting the beasts keep moving, and started toward Eli, lifting his bullwhip shoulder high until Eli stepped forward and said, "You try that and I'll have to take it from you and hide you with it!"

The man growled, cocked back his arm and started to let it fly, but Eli charged him, head down and buried his head in the man's chest, driving him back into the oxen and dropping him to the ground. As he stumbled, pushing away from the oxen, Eli snatched the whip from his hand and stepped back, coiling the blacksnake bull-whip as he did, lifting the corner of his lip in a snarl, "There's nothing I hate more than a bully like you that thinks he can make others into cowards!" He flipped the popper behind him and brought the whip forward. It whispered through the air and cut across the bully's shoulder, ripping the back of his shirt and marking his skin. Eli snatched it back again and stepped further back as the big man lowered his head to charge. Eli tossed the whip aside and as the beast of a man charged, arms outstretched and growling, Eli stepped to the side, dropped his hand behind the man's neck, brought his knee up to smash his face, and with his left hand shoved the man away.

The bullwhacker stumbled to the side, tripped on his own feet and fell, both hands on his face as he whimpered. He pulled his hands away, both covered with blood and looked up at Eli who stood, hands on hips, grinning.

"So, bully boy, you want some more, or do you want to catch up to your freighter and the oxen?"

The big man rolled to his side, staggered up, and glared at Eli as he held his face with one hand, grabbed his whip with the other, and stumbled toward his wagon that never slowed. He grabbed the side braces, used it to help him walk, and without a look back to the others, was soon lost in the dust of the rest of the wagons.

Moses came alongside, "Suh, that was the best whuppin' I seen a man git since, well, since we was in th' ahmy!"

# CHAPTER 9

## PALOUSE

E li and Donna stretched out ahead of the wagons, scouting the land and road before them, when Donna asked, "Will we be traveling with the wagons all the way to Walla Walla?"

Eli shrugged as he glanced to the woman, "Prob'ly. It'll be safer for everyone that way, I think."

She looked long at Eli, wondering about the man and if their futures might be intertwined. She had no idea what she might do in Walla Walla for during the time she spent there before, she trusted Hank to provide for them, but she had to help out by singing in one of the bigger taverns in town. That was not a life she wanted for herself, but with limited education and experience, opportunities for a single woman were rare. She glanced at Eli again, wondering about him and his plans, although she knew he was on the hunt for his boys, he still had to have money, and how would he pay for supplies for his search? She had heard him talk about his family shipbuilding business and that he had been a career military man, but what now? She looked his way again, smiling to herself and thinking, *At least he's a good-lookin' rascal.*

The sun was resting on the tips of the tall hemlock and fir as they pushed across the river. Eli had left the road to make their crossing at a gravel ripple rather than the sloping banks and deeper water of the road. They were just downstream from a dogleg bend in the river, and Eli's chosen camp was within sight of the road. Donna said, "This is the Palouse River, the road follows it, sorta, all the way to the Snake River, down south a spell."

"I thought it might be the Palouse," replied Eli, as Rusty climbed the bank of the river, stopped, and shook off the excess as he turned to look at the grey and Donna on her palomino. The big stallion had assumed his role as herd stallion and was especially interested in the palomino mare of Donna's. Eli moved toward the trees, spoke over his shoulder, "We'll make camp here. There's room for the wagons yonder, they can see this from the road, and you can listen for them, wave 'em over, and," he glanced to the lowering sun, "there's time for me to try and find some fresh meat."

"While you do that, I might wash out some clothes, maybe start on supper," she laughed, "Don't I sound like a real housewife!"

Eli grinned, looking sidelong at her, but dropping his eyes as he stepped down and ground tied Rusty and led the grey closer to the trees where he would picket the packhorse and Donna's palomino. He stripped the gear from the packhorse, stacked the panniers and parfleche under the trees and after stripping the gear from the palomino, picketed the yellow horse near the grey.

"It looks like the river takes to the trees downstream, might find some deer coming for their evening drink," he spoke from his saddle as Donna stood near, "shouldn't be too long and the wagons'll be here soon."

"I'll be fine, thank you."

————

Eli disappeared into the trees and willows and Donna stood, hands on hips, as she looked around, feeling all alone and a little wary. She had become accustomed to the comforting presence and safety of being with Eli, and the quiet of the woods with only the chuckling of the stream nearby seemed so empty. She took a deep breath, dropped her hands, and went to the packs to fetch the utensils and other makings for their supper, and once that was laid out, she dug in the bedrolls and packs for clothing that could use some washing.

With a big bar of lye soap in one hand, an armload of clothing in the other, she went to water's edge where some backwater offered both rocks and deep water for washing. With a look around, she waded into the shallows, sat the soap and most of the clothes on a big rock and began her work. She was close to finishing, when she heard the sounds of the approaching wagons and stood to look to the road. She waved, and when the first wagon waved back, she continued with the wash. Moses rode into the camp, came to the river's edge, "Howdy ma'am, Eli around?"

"He went hunting," nodding downstream, "should be back soon. He's hopin' to get enough for everyone, so…" she shrugged, shading her eyes from the sun's rays bouncing off the ripples.

"If'n you need anythin' ma'am, just give a hollah!" chuckled Moses as he reined the horse around.

"Will do, but I'm sure he'll be back real soon," answered Donna, scrubbing the shirt she had worn when she first met Eli. As she finished with each item she tossed it onto the grass on the shore, and when done, she waded back and began laying everything out on the willows to dry.

Satisfied with her work, she stepped back, looked at the clothes-covered bushes, and smiled, shook her head slightly and started back to the camp to finish preparing the fire and more for supper. The sounds of other wagons came from the near side of the river and Donna stood, looking about and through the trees, saw two wagons coming from the south with several outriders. The wagons pulled off the road on the far side, the riders turning to the trees and the clearing beside the river, apparently making their camp. She glanced to the nearby wagons of their friends, and all were busy setting up their camp and paying little heed to the newcomers, but Donna had a chill crawl up her back and did not like what she was feeling.

As she busied herself about the camp, she thought of the newcomers, and did not want to even look that direction and tried to keep herself out of their sight. She knew most men in the West were good men, but she also knew how men, whenever they were away from their women or families and around only men, they were not as honorable as they were in town or around their women. It had something to do with the wildness of the territory, the mountains, and the absence of law and accountability. She also knew that all it would take is just one man to take the lead and whatever he did the others would easily follow, unless there were those that could stand against the wrongdoer. She looked to the trees and the river, hoping to see Eli, but nothing moved, no big stallion was heard.

She rose from the fireside, stood, and glanced to the other camp, and saw a big man looking her way. She dropped her eyes and turned back to the horses, making busy and staying out of sight. But she heard a shout from the far camp, looked over the back of her palomino and saw three men craning around to look to her camp, talking to one another until the big man started across the road, waving the others to follow, and that was what concerned her, when men have to have a group for their misdeeds. Donna touched the pistol at her back, her loose jacket hiding it from view, but still easily reached. She ducked behind the palomino, and with a handful of grass, began giving the horse a rubdown, trying not to look at the men.

The three men stopped at the edge of the camp, the big man standing with arms crossed over his barrel chest, and called out, "Hey, you! You there with the horses! Show yourself!"

Donna looked over the back of her palomino, showing only the top of her head and face, "What do you want?"

"Come out here so we can see you!" he demanded.

"Get out of here and leave me alone!" she ordered, doing her best to sound unafraid.

"What'chu doin' out here alone? Or are you with them coloreds?" growled the big man.

Donna tiptoed to look over the back of her horse and saw movement behind the three would-be ruffians. There was no mistaking the big form of Moses, but behind him were several others. Moses jacked a round into the magazine of his new Henry rifle and the unmistakable ratcheting sound turned the three men around to face Moses and three of the men. Moses looked like a barrel of a man in his bib overalls, even bigger than the blowhard, but the men with him were also intimidating, not just because they each held rifles across their chests, but two of the men had uniform trousers of the Union cavalry, and the third had a uniform jacket with three gold stripes. One glance told the three interlopers they were facing experienced fighting soldiers, and none were smiling.

The blustery bully growled, "What'chu want? This don' concern you'ns!"

Moses just slowly nodded his head and with the muzzle of his rifle, he motioned the men away. As he did, two of the other men beside him also jacked a round into the chambers of their rifles, the clatter of the levers and actions speaking louder than any words.

The would-be bully had lost his bluster and looked to his partners and back to the soldiers, he growled and mumbled, and started back to their camp across the road. Donna breathed a deep sigh of relief and stepped from behind her horse, smiling to Moses, and said, "Thank you, Moses, men," she looked from one to the other, smiling and nodding slightly.

"But ma'am, we din't do nothin'. We just went for a little walk and was gonna do some target shootin' with muh new rifle mister Eli done give me!" he chuckled with a deep rumbling belly laugh. Moses nodded to the trees, "Here come the colonel now, ma'am, so I reckon there's no need to be tellin' him what happened. Don' want him gettin' upset and whuppin' another man, now do we?"

"Prob'ly not, Moses. But stick around, he prob'ly has some meat for you!" she smiled, looking at the men and back to see Eli and the big stallion come from the trees.

Behind the cantle bounced the carcass of a mule deer and Eli called out as he waved to Moses, "Got some fresh meat, Moses!"

# CHAPTER 10

## SCABLANDS

With the sun at their back, Eli and Donna rode beside Moses as the Mullan Road pointed west. Long shadows stretched before them only to be met by an early morning warm wind. The further they traveled, the drier the land became, showing buff-colored grasses, sagebrush, and little else. The Palouse River had bent to the north, but the road continued west. Above the wind that had become incessantly hot and aggravating, Eli called to Donna, "How far to water?"

"I don't know! Maybe half a day. After that it's further still!" she shouted to be heard above the howl of the wind.

They rode with heads ducked and hats tied down. Eli reined up and lifted his neckerchief over his nose and mouth, looked to Donna to see she had already covered her face, and to Moses who was also lifting his neckerchief. The blowing silt masked the sun and was doing its best to hide the road, but the horses plodded on, heads down. After the first couple hours, Eli reined up on the lee side of a low mound and motioned the others to stop as well. He grabbed his canteen and wet a rag and began to wipe out the noses of the claybank and the grey. Donna stood beside her palomino stroking her neck, and Eli wiped the mare's nose clean. He looked at Donna, "If this wind doesn't let up, we'll have to do this 'bout every hour or so or stop."

Moses had used his hat to give his mount a drink and Eli did the same for their horses. Moses had squatted on his haunches, lifted a handful of the fine silt, let it run through his fingers, looked at Eli, "This'd be fine soil fer growin' things if'n there was any water."

Eli chuckled, "If there was any water, it's nothin' but silt now!" He looked to the sky, the dingy dust cloud still obscuring the sun. He looked at Moses, "You think you might need to check on the wagons, make sure they're tendin' to the horses?"

"Nah'suh, them fellas know whut to do, an' muh missus'll keep the boy in line, make him tend to 'em," chuckled Moses, rising to climb aboard his mount. Eli and Donna stepped back aboard and pointed the horses west on the road and with heads ducked, they continued on the way.

It was late afternoon when the horses smelled the water and quickened their pace. The wind had been intermittent, but the dusty silt lay deep on the road and every footfall brought a puff of dust rising. A dark line showed the green of the river and even the wind seemed to pause for a deep breath. After the tiresome day of fighting the wind, everyone looked the same with dust on their clothes, in their hair, and covering any exposed areas of their face. Eli looked at Moses, laughed, "Looks like we're all the same color now!"

Moses let the deep rumble come with a smile, and he

nodded, "Yessuh, we is. Sho' be nice if'n it was always thisaway and then mebbe folks'd be nicer to one'nother."

"You're sure right about that, Moses. But for now, let's get the horses tended to and then we can take turns with the womenfolk and see if we can turn that river into mud!" laughed Eli.

———

THE NEXT TWO days the wind was a little more merciful and only came in gusts, but still it carried the fine silt and even obscured the road in places by drifting like snow in the wintertime. The road was nowhere near water and the hot sun and blowing silt made travel miserable, but late on the second day after their last water, the rolling hills and flat-topped buttes pushed back and let the Palouse River change its course from west to south and the greenery of the river beckoned the travelers for a day of rest. With bathing, clothes washing, and filling water barrels, the day of rest was more a day of cleaning, especially for the womenfolk. But the men took the opportunity to hunt for fresh meat and they were fortunate to take their first buffalo. As they were busy at the butchering, Moses looked to Eli, "We never got close 'nuff 'fore, an' well, I wa'n't too sure 'bout tryin' to get one o' these big'uns all by muh lonesome. The herd we saw was," he waved his arm side to side, "so big, it covered the whole land. An' I din't wanna start no stampede an' get runned o'er."

Eli chuckled, "You were smart about that, Moses. It takes a lot to stampede a herd of buffalo, but once they get movin' they churn up everything in their path and nothing could survive. But," he grinned as he slipped his big Bowie knife through the hide and with edge up, began splitting the beast from tail to tongue, "there'll be good eating tonight!" He chuckled as he thought, "Now, if we were Natives, Sioux or Blackfoot, we wouldn't be doin' this 'cuz this is woman's work!"

Moses paused, frowning, "You mean to say, them folks have the women do this?"

"Ummhmm," nodded Eli, "all the men do is kill 'em, maybe split 'em open to get the liver, and dip the liver in the bile and eat it raw!"

Moses frowned, leaned back and with a snarl shook his head, "Nosuh, if'n it ain't cooked, I ain't eatin' it!"

———

THE EARLY MORNING sky arched clear and blue as they pushed across the Palouse River and continued west. Eli and Donna rode alone and the land lay flat before them with the rolling hills that had been commonplace, but random buttes and flat-topped mesas stood as sentinels to the prairie of sagebrush, buffalo grass, and cacti. The mesas, most showing basaltic rimrock, the taller mesas with talus slopes, but nothing that showed water. Throughout the tireless flats, random clusters of dark basaltic rock lay as if the Creator had tossed a handful of leftovers in a pile, or scattered the excess as if broadcasting seeds.

Eli recognized the basalt as the remnants of ancient volcanic activity, but the silt must have been from an ancient flood. He let a slow grin tug at his mouth as he remembered the biblical account of the flood that covered the earth in the days of Noah and nodded his understanding of the ways of God. Donna saw his expression and frowned as she asked, "Are you talking to yourself?"

He laughed, "No, just remembering."

"Remembering? What?"

"What the Bible said about an ancient flood, when God flooded the world and had Noah build an ark."

"What would make you think of that?"

He grinned, pointed to the fine silt that showed in drifts along the road, "See that?"

"See it? We've been eating it for days!" she declared, shaking her head and not understanding what this man was doing.

"Ummhmm, but that's a fine silt that only shows when there is a flood, that's what water does to dirt and rocks, turns it into a fine silt."

Donna frowned, looking down at the silt as the horses plodded along, back to Eli, "So, you're saying there was a flood long ago that made that?"

"Ummhmm," he pointed at a nearby butte with a rim of rock that appeared to be hexagonal pillars, "and that rock, that's basalt and it's from a long-ago volcano, before the flood and the flood might have come right after and cooled the rock and began covering it with the silt."

Donna shook her head, "And all this time I was thinking those rock piles and ridges reminded me of scabs, you know, like when you skin your knees or something and a scab forms and gets all dark and hard before you start pickin' away at it?"

Eli looked around, "Yeah, I can see why you'd think that. Kinda like scabs on the land that show of what the land has suffered in years gone by, umhmm."

MIDAFTERNOON on the last day of the week out of their first crossing of the Palouse River they were nearing the confluence of the Palouse and the Snake Rivers. Eli and Donna were riding scout out ahead of the wagons and with rolling hills on their right and the distant sound of roaring river on their left, Eli moved off the road and started toward what appeared to be the shoulders of a canyon. Sagebrush marched down the long slope before them and turned their heads south toward the confluence as Eli crossed the basin and took to the shoulder of the gorge of the Palouse. He stepped down as the roar of waters reverberated up from the deep gorge, and as Donna held his crooked elbow, he leaned forward to look over the edge at the crashing whitewater below and feel the fine mist rising from the gorge.

"Oh, that's beautiful!" declared Donna, gripping his arm a bit tighter.

"Ummhmm, and you can see the layers of the basaltic rock on the far side, standing up like they're watching over the entire gorge," stated Eli. "That hollow seems to magnify the sound."

"It scares me," said Donna, pulling herself closer to Eli.

He glanced down at her and turned back from the edge, "We better get goin' so we can make arrangements for the wagons on the ferry."

Donna looked at Eli, wondering why he always seemed to pull away from her whenever they were close. She sighed, and mounted her palomino and followed Eli back to the road that would take them to the confluence and the ferry.

# CHAPTER 11

## WALLA WALLA

The sun was warm on his back as he sat atop the little knoll, knees drawn up and supporting his elbows as he used the binoculars to scan the valley below. "Looks like they got 'em some good farms down there, an' these over here," motioning to his left, "have some sizable wheat fields. Didn't expect to see that!" declared Eli.

"Them down yonder," began Moses, pointing to the western edge of the settlement, "looks to be fine farms, too."

"The town 'pears to be good sized, reckon maybe a thousand or so folks. That creek runs right through the town" explained Eli as he handed the binoculars to Moses.

"Yahsuh, tha's a big town alright. But I like them farms an' I know muh folks will be mighty glad to see that. Gives 'em hope, it do," drawled Moses as he focused on the farms downstream from the town.

Eli stood, stretched, "You wanna go into town right

away, or…" asked Eli, as the two started back to the wagons.

"Nosuh, I think we'll find us a place to camp, settle in a mite, wait till mawnin' to go into town," explained Moses.

"Well, I'm goin' to get me and Donna some rooms at the hotel, maybe get a bath and some clean clothes, and have dinner in a restaurant," he chuckled. "How about we meet up at the general store, say, 'bout eight in the morning?"

"That'd be fine, Colonel, yessuh."

———

"WELL, THAT'S A GOOD THING," declared Eli as he folded the *Washington Statesman* newspaper and sat it beside his now empty plate. He smiled at Donna who was finishing her cake, enjoying every bite.

"What's a good thing?" she asked, dabbing at the corners of her mouth with a napkin. They both were enjoying the time together in the popular Mill Creek Café, just down the street from the Bon Ton Hotel where they had rooms.

"Congress passed the Fourteenth Amendment, it'll keep the Civil Rights Bill in force in all the states, once it's ratified that is."

"Alright, you'll have to explain that to me," she said, putting her napkin back on her lap and reaching for the coffee cup that rested on its fine china saucer.

"The Civil Rights Act gives every born American the right to all the privileges of any other, basically that's what Moses and his friends are counting on to be able to homestead some property for farms they couldn't before. But, some states, mainly in the South, want to pass laws against that and the Fourteenth Amendment will keep it intact and guarantee those rights," explained Eli, lifting his cup of steaming coffee for a sip.

"I see, does that also apply to women?" smiled Donna.

"I believe so," answered Eli. "Why, you have something in mind?"

She casually looked around the restaurant, counted the tables and the customers, smiled at Eli, "You have been bragging on my cooking for the last week or more, and maybe I'd do better having a café or something like that instead of singing for a crowd of unruly men."

Eli cocked his head to the side, squinted his eyes a little as he looked at Donna. She was a beautiful woman now that she was cleaned up, fixed up and more, but could she run a business? In all their conversations, she had shown a natural curiosity, and intelligence. She got along well with just about everyone, except those she thought needed shooting. He chuckled to himself, thinking about the possibilities. He had planned to leave her here in Walla Walla, but now that he knew her better, he was concerned about her welfare and future, although she had expressed interest in sharing his future, he was not ready for that. He knew she did not have the wherewithal to buy a business, at least he did not think so, but he could help with that, and he would feel better about leaving her behind if she had a home and more.

Donna frowned, "What are you thinking? You look like you're planning some great something or other. You're not planning on robbing the bank or something like that, are you?"

Eli chuckled, "Do you really think I'd do something like that?"

"Well, no, but you looked so serious."

"Just thinkin' about what you said about having a restaurant or some other business."

She smiled, lifted her head haughtily, "I think I would be a good businesswoman. And I just happen to know the owner of this restaurant."

"You do?" asked Eli, showing a bit of incredulity on his face.

"Yes! His name is Homer Singletary," she glanced to the doorway to the kitchen, "and that's him coming right there!" She smiled and gave a little wave to the man exiting the kitchen, a long apron over his front and tied at his waist. The man was visiting with the diners and going from table to table. When he neared their table, he smiled broadly, held out his hand, and said, "Donna, dear Donna, I did not expect to see you here again! I thought you and what's his name…" He laughed as he took her hand in his and held it as he spoke, totally ignoring Eli.

Donna smiled up at the man. "You know his name, Homer, don't give me that!" she declared, laughing. She turned to Eli, and glanced back. "Homer, I want you to meet a friend of mine. This is Elijah McCain. Eli, this is Homer Singletary."

Homer turned to face Eli, extended his hand as he smiled, "Mr. McCain, pleased to meet you, sir. Any friend of Donna's is a friend of mine."

Eli asked the man to join them, and they visited a short while about Hank and Donna's failed venture to the goldfields, the business of Walla Walla and more, until Eli asked, "Do you know a man they call Six? He's a freighter, I believe."

Homer smiled, "Know him well. Whenever he is in town, he always eats here. Although he gives the appearance of a gruffy muleskinner, he's actually a very shrewd businessman and a hard worker, that one. He's a good man, and he will probably be here for his breakfast right after we open up in the morning." Homer glanced from Eli to Donna and back, "You need to talk business with him?"

Eli reached into his inside pocket and extracted the tintype he always carried, held it out to Homer, "Those are my sons, Jubal and Joshua Paine. The last I heard, they were working for him, and I've been on their trail for some time."

Homer frowned, "They in trouble?"

Eli grinned, "No, no trouble. I promised their mother I would find them and ask them to return home. They left the army, came west hunting gold and adventure, and I've tracked them from Kentucky to here."

"I never saw them, but the last time Six was in here, he was grumbling about some of his help leaving him and going downriver on a riverboat that was bound for the mouth of the Columbia. Dunno if it was them, but I'm sure he'll tell you if you find him in the morning," explained Homer, looking around the restaurant, "But now, I've got to get back to work," he rose, looked back at the two, "See you in the morning?"

Donna smiled and answered, "We'll be here!"

She looked at Eli, "What are you gonna do if the boys took the riverboat?"

Eli shook his head, dropped his eyes, and answered, "Dunno. If they're on a boat, there's no telling how far they'll go, if they'll come back this way, or..." he shrugged. "I know they know I'm looking for them. When they were in the Last Chance Gulch area, we had a mutual acquaintance that told them I was looking for them, but they did not wait around or try to find me, but they did go back to the mountains, looking for gold. So,

I'm not too sure they want to be found, at least not anytime soon."

He lapsed into a moment of memories, thinking about the boys, knowing he had spent so little time with them. He was a West Point graduate and career army officer that kept him from time at home. The boys' mother had been the wife of one of his close friends and classmates and Eli had promised to take care of her and the baby when his friend died in Eli's arms. Because she was expecting, he stepped in to become her husband and the father of the baby who turned out to be twin boys. During the war, they had joined the Union Army, but disillusioned, they deserted and came west, searching for gold and a new life. Eli knew they probably thought their "by-the-book" father was after them because they deserted, but he only wanted to fulfill the deathbed promise to their mother, to bring them home. It just seemed that one promise begets another promise and more.

Donna interrupted his reverie with a question, "What about Moses and the others?"

Eli frowned, "What about them?"

"Are you going to help them to continue west, find the land they want to make into farms?"

He reached for his coffee cup just as the waitress came with a pot to fill it, he watched as the black brew filled his cup and thanked the woman, picked up the cup and took a deep draught, looked over the rim at Donna, "Probably, if they need the help. But they've come this far without me and I'm sure they're quite capable of going all the way."

"Yes, but, well, you just seem to be such a help to them, and some people aren't too kind to coloreds."

"That's true. Shouldn't be that way, but it is, that's

why I'm glad to see the Civil Rights Act and the Four-teenth Amendment making its way. I've heard some grumbling among some folks that next the coloreds will be getting to vote, and maybe even women!"

Donna's eyes flared as she smiled, "Now *that* would be a good thing. If we women could vote, we'd get things straightened out in a hurry!" she laughed.

Eli shook his head, looked over the rim of the coffee cup and used it to hide his smile.

# CHAPTER 12

## BUSINESS

The Mill Creek Café was busy, all but two tables were taken when Eli and Donna stepped through the door. Homer was behind the counter, nodded when they came in and motioned to one of the tables for them to be seated. Eli held the chair for Donna to be seated, sat down opposite her, and looked up to see Homer bringing a man with him to their table. He looked at Eli, "You said you wanted to meet Six, here he is!" He turned to the man at his side, "This is the man I told you about," and turned away to return to his work, leaving the man standing alone. Eli stood, extended his hand, "I'm Eli McCain and this is Donna Kennedy. Won't you join us?"

"I'm known as Six, although my full name is Sid Six, but most folks call me Six because of this," he lifted his hand to show the six fingers. After the handshakes and introductions, Six seated himself and looked to Eli, "I'm afraid you have me at a disadvantage, Mr. McCain. Just what is it you need from me, are you looking for a freighter?"

Eli handed Six the tintype, "Know those two?" he asked, watching the reaction of the man.

"Why you lookin' for 'em, they in trouble or sumpin'?" he asked.

"No, no trouble," and Eli continued to explain about his search for the boys and his promise to their mother. "I know they have worked on riverboats, freighters, and such and the last word I had was they were seen with your mule train on the Mullan Road."

"Yes, they were. Good workers, no complaints. They said when they signed on that they might leave when they got here, maybe take a job on a riverboat or somethin'. Said they were done with the goldfields, thinkin' 'bout savin' up and gettin' into business of some sort. I told 'em to look me up if they came back upriver, and they said they would."

They spent the time over breakfast getting acquainted, talking about the territory, the trail over the passes and more, until Six looked at Eli, "You were an officer in the war?"

"That's right. I mustered out as a lieutenant colonel, served under Sheridan, commanding a cavalry unit."

"Have you got plans for the next, oh, two, three months?"

Eli told about the wagons of Moses and company, and Six nodded as he began to explain. "I need a good man, one I can depend on no matter what, to go with me and my freighters over Naches Trail to Puget Sound and the coast. Part of my cargo is to go by ship down to the coast to San Francisco. Now, I've got good muleskinners and roustabouts, good equipment, but I need somebody to scout the way, maybe do a little hunting for meat and such. Interested? Pays good!"

"What about the wagons of my friends? I kinda promised them I'd help them."

"You say they have five wagons and they're all ex-army?"

"That's right."

"Bring 'em along. The Palouse and the Yakima have been a little restless lately and having more guns would be a help. And if they find a place they want to stake out, then so be it."

Eli looked at Sid, glanced to Donna, and said, "I've got to meet them at the general store, and I'll talk about it. When you leavin'?"

"Day after tomorrow," answered Sid.

Eli looked at Donna and back to Sid, "Alright, I'll walk you," looking at Donna, "back to the hotel and then I'll meet Moses at the store." He looked at Sid, "I'm at the Bon Ton if you need to talk. We'll probably be back here for supper, so, maybe we can talk more then?"

"That'd be fine," answered Sid, standing to shake hands with Eli.

But Donna remained seated and looked up at Eli, "You go ahead. I want to stay and talk with Homer as soon as things slack up a bit. I might even help him, I haven't seen his waitress around so…" she shrugged, smiling at Eli.

Eli chuckled, glanced to Six, "I learned a long time ago to never argue with a woman." He looked at Donna, "Then I'll see you back at the hotel. I might go to the camp with the men and talk, then I'll be back. If you're not there, I will assume you will be here." He looked at Six, "You want to meet back here for supper, say seven?"

Sid grinned, "That'll be fine. I'll see you then."

———

SCHWABACHER BROTHERS STORE was the primary business in the growing town of Walla Walla. It was a combination grocer, clothes store, and general supply store for the area. Would-be gold miners outfitted here before taking their wagons over the Mullan Road to the goldfields of Montana, farmers bought their equipment and supplies here, and most residents purchased all their needs here. Eli stepped to the boardwalk before the store and was surprised to see Moses, Matthew, and Ezra, all with their uniform blouses on and grinning ear to ear as they saw Eli. Moses was the first, but the others quickly followed, to salute the colonel, and Eli chuckled, returned the salute, and shook hands with each one. "So, why the uniforms?"

"Well suh, we found most folks are mo' tolerable of us when we is in uniform. Mo' likely to let us buy supplies an' such," answered Moses.

Eli frowned, shook his head but knew there was nothing he could say, and asked the men, "So, camp alright last night?"

"Yessuh," answered Ezra Conklin. "We even talked to a farmer, right nice fella, who tol' us about the land, crops an' such. Even invited us to homestead 'roun 'chere. Said they was lots a land, an' there's some that's even doin' what he called 'dryland' farmin', where they don't have no water 'cepin' the rain." He shook his head, "I dunno 'bout that, this hyar seems to be mighty dry country."

The four men stepped into the store and were somewhat surprised at the goods that were stacked on counters, against the wall, in barrels and crates, display cases, and racks on the wall. They looked about as they stood just inside, and at the encouragement of a man behind the counter, "Come in! Come in! Look around an' I'll be right with you!" They would soon learn the speaker was Sigmond Schwabacher, one of the brothers that owned the business.

Each man had a list of goods and presented the list to the man behind the counter. He looked at each list, looked at each man, and asked the group, "Are you men from the fort?"

Moses spoke up, "No suh, we done mustered out and are travelin' wit' our families. Goin' west to find us some good farmland. That's why we need the supplies."

The man slowly nodded, looked at the men again and handed off the lists to one of his clerks and spoke to Moses, "My helper will get your goods together. Feel free to look around, you might find something you need that is not on your list."

Moses was surprised at the congeniality of the man, looked to his companions and to Eli, and started to look around. Eli stepped beside him, and asked, "Do all the men have good rifles? You know, like a Spencer or Henry or Winchester? A repeater type?"

Moses thought about it a moment, looked at Eli, "All but McCoslin. He's still usin' the Springfield he was issued. But th' others have good uns."

Eli spoke softly to Moses, "Make sure they get plenty of ammunition. If they don't have the money, I'll help, but you might need it further west."

Moses frowned, but nodded, trusting the judgment of his one-time commanding officer. He spoke to the others, each man adding additional ammunition for his weapons, and wondering just what they might be encountering further on the trip. Eli added a used Henry rifle and additional ammunition to his order as well and once done, the men starting packing goods outside.

Moses had brought one of the wagons into town and the goods were loaded aboard.

"I'll get my horse and come with you. I'd like to see those farms you were talkin' about," offered Eli after loading his goods in the wagon with the others. He fetched his horse and the packhorse, followed the wagon out of town and at the campsite beside the Walla Walla River just west of town, he gathered the men together to talk about the trip ahead. He explained about the freighter, the possibility of hostile Indians, and the difficult pass. But he also spoke about the fertile farmland on both sides of the mountains, the ranches they would pass, and the farmland that might be promising.

Moses looked around the circle, looked at Eli, "I think I speak for all of us. I likes the idea of having mo' men if we was to be attacked by the Indians, an' if'n we find land 'fore we gits to th' other side o' them mountains, that'd be fine too." He looked at the others, each man nodding, most grinning. With a nod, he answered, "So, if'n you be goin', I reckon we is, too!"

# CHAPTER 13

## DISCUSSIONS

The smithy at the livery grinned when Eli returned. "Thot you'd be back, din't think it'd be this soon, but them stalls are still empty. Put'm away, give 'em some grain if'n yore of a mind." He turned back to his forge, glanced up at Eli, "You gonna need 'em come mornin'?"

"Not for another day, then I'll be pullin' out 'fore first light," explained Eli as he stripped the gear from the horses. He had loaded his supplies on the packhorse and stacked it all in the corner of the stall for the grey with the panniers and other gear. As he walked out, the smithy waved, and Eli stepped into the light. He walked the length of Main Street to get to the Bon Ton Hotel, looking at the businesses and passing the people, most friendly. It was the typical Western town, the buildings with the false front façade, most signs crudely painted, boardwalk stretching the length of the block. He saw the Pioneer Meat Market, the newspaper office for the *Washington Statesman*, Emil Meyer's City Brewery and Bakery, two other hotels, a bathhouse and shaving salon, liquor store, two cafés, and five saloons that sandwiched a bookstore in the middle of the block. He chuckled as he stepped up to the door of the hotel and pushed through to step into the simply appointed parlor. Donna was sitting on the settee by the window and stood as he entered, a broad smile showing and her hand waving him over.

They sat together and she grabbed his hand, anxious to tell him her news. He grinned as she began, "You know how you said it would be good for me to have a business? Well, Homer has the gold bug and he's wanting to unload his restaurant as soon as possible!" she declared, bouncing on the settee with excitement.

"Well, I suppose that's good news, but…"

"No, no, let me explain," she interrupted, "it's not just good news, it's a real possibility." She looked around to see if anyone was nearby and back to Eli, "He wants out and he's in a hurry. He said if he can get enough money to outfit him to go to the goldfields, he would give a note for the balance! Isn't that good?" she asked, anxious for his answer.

"That depends on what he wants for the business, and how much the business makes, and what you would need to do to take it over, and if you think you could, and…" he shrugged when he saw he was dampening her spirits.

Her forehead wrinkled and she sat back, dropping his hands and looking at him, "I thought you would be excited for me!"

Eli grinned, "Well, I think it would be a possibility that we could talk about. But for right now, I need to change clothes and we're supposed to go back to the restaurant to meet with Six and maybe then we can talk a little more with Homer. How's that sound?" he asked, reaching for her hand.

She leaned toward him, a slight smile replacing the frown and slowly nodded. "I'm counting on you and your business judgment. You know how most men are, they think a woman doesn't have the smarts to handle business matters and I admit, I don't have the experience, but I know what works and what doesn't, and I think this might be a good opportunity."

"Then, we'll just talk a little more with Homer and decide, but first," he said as he rose from the settee and nodded to the stairs, "I need to change."

————

DONNA TUCKED her hand in the crook of Eli's elbow as they stepped off the stoop of the Bon Ton Hotel and started down the boardwalk. Both the hotel and the Mill Creek Café were at the west end of Main Street with the back doors facing Mill Creek. The café was the westernmost eating place and the first that any visitors coming from the boats or freighters on the Columbia River would see and the café had an established reputation for good food with the boatmen and others. Donna and Eli were casually strolling on the boardwalk when a group of men pushed open the door of the café and stumbled out onto the boardwalk, almost bumping into Donna. Eli stepped forward to protect her, but the man staggered back, grabbed his hat, "'Scuse me, ma'am! Didn't see you there. Me shipmates have been nippin' the bot'l an're not too steady. We don' have our land legs yet." He stumbled back to the others who had stopped and were staring at Donna.

Donna dropped her eyes and mumbled, "You're

excused, thank you," and turned to Eli, who had slipped his hand inside his jacket and grasped the butt of the Colt holstered at his hip. He glared at the men, noticing the bulges in their shirts that told of the presence of belaying pins and recognized these men as experienced sailors, although they were undoubtedly from the steamboats at the dock below town. He held himself in check and stepped up to put himself between the men and Donna. He opened the door with his left hand and looked over his shoulder at the men as Donna stepped into the café, followed closely by Eli.

The crowd had thinned out and there were several tables empty. A waving hand caught Eli's attention and he nudged Donna toward the table in the corner where Sid and Homer sat together, nursing cups of coffee. The men stood when Donna neared and Eli pulled out the chair to seat her, shook hands with both men and seated himself.

Sid was anxious for Eli's answer, and asked, "Did you talk to the others?"

"I did, and they're wanting to join up with you and your freighters. You say we'll be leaving day after tomorrow?"

"That's right, and that's good news. I take it you're coming as well?" asked Sid.

"I think so, seems like that's what I oughta do," he drawled as he looked from Sid to Donna and then to Homer. He turned to Homer, "Donna tells me you've got the gold fever and are lookin' to take off to Montana Territory."

Homer dropped his head, mumbled, "Hadn't thought of it like that, but, yeah, I'd like to try my luck in the goldfields. I've been hearing some good reports from around Bear Gulch and the area thereabouts, some big strikes."

"Well," began Eli, looking at Donna and back to Homer, "we came for dinner. Sid said he was buyin' so, I'm hungry! What's your special?"

"I've got some good beef from rancher Splawn so I can serve you up a steak and some home-grown potatoes from one o' the farmers down the valley hereabouts," offered Homer, standing to go to the kitchen.

"That'll be fine, make mine medium rare and," he looked to Donna, his eyebrows lifted in a question, and she nodded, "hers the same."

———

WHEN DINNER WAS FINISHED and the coffee cups filled, they pushed back from the table and Homer joined them again. Eli asked, "So, Donna tells me she's interested in your business," and the three lapsed into a question-and-answer session discussing the business and the possibilities of the café changing hands. When the questions had been asked and answered, Eli and Donna excused themselves with Eli explaining, "We need to talk about this but it's interesting. Since Sid and his group are not leaving for another day, I've got some things to get ready and we," nodding to Donna, "need to talk a bit, so, we'll get together tomorrow."

"That sounds good," answered Homer as he stood to shake hands with Eli and to bid Donna a good-night.

———

THEY WALKED IN SILENCE, the moon lighting the way and a few windows laying squares of light across the walk. Eli heard sounds of movement from the dark alleyway beside the hotel and pulled Donna a little closer, whispering to her, "I think there's somebody in the alley between the buildings there," nodding beside the hotel.

When they stepped past the lighted window of the building next to the hotel, a voice growled from the darkness, "Hold it right there, matey!" and Eli stepped between Donna and the alleyway, lifting his jacket for Donna to see the LeMat pistol at his back. He felt her slip the pistol free as he lifted the Colt from the holster at his hip, but kept it obscured under the fold of his jacket. Two men stepped forward and Eli recognized them as two of the deckhands from the riverboat that had accosted them before, but now they held belaying pins before them, slapping them into the palms of their hands. "If'n you don' want your head bashed in, you'll give us your money and the woman."

Eli pretended to reach into an inner pocket with his left hand, but quickly brought the Colt out, cocking the hammer as he did, "And if you don't want to have a hole through your middle, you'll back off!" demanded Eli.

The first man started to lift his pin but the clicking of another hammer being cocked made him look to see Donna, slightly beside and behind Eli, holding the LeMat and smiling, "Now boys, I know you'd like me to come with you, but I think I'll stay with my man here. But if you want me to show you how well I can shoot..." she shrugged, grinning.

"Uh, uh, no, no..." mumbled the men, starting to back away until Eli said, "Drop those belaying pins right there!" motioning with the muzzle of his Colt.

Both men dropped the hardwood pins, quickly turned and disappeared into the darkness. Donna giggled, "Mr.

McCain, I have more fun with you!" and handed him the LeMat. "I had no idea you had so many weapons about you," she laughed. Eli holstered the Colt, bent to pick up the pins, and Donna asked, "What are those things?" a frown painting her face.

"Belaying pins. They're used on sailing vessels, schooners, sloops and such. They use 'em to tie off the ropes from the sails and more." He held one out for Donna to examine and she was surprised at the size and heft of the pin, measuring about eighteen inches long, with a rounded end shaped much like a bat, and the long pin end straight. "That would have hurt!" she declared, handing the pin back to Eli as they walked into the hotel lobby.

# CHAPTER 14

## YAKIMA

Donna stood beside the big stallion of Eli, her hand on his knee, "I don't know how I can ever thank you, Eli."

He smiled down at the dark-haired beauty, "You put in your savings, and I invested in what I think will be a good business. I'll be coming back to check on my investment and I'm expecting to see this café busier than ever."

She smiled up at him, "You know you will! Do you know how long you'll be gone?"

"Don't rightly know, maybe two, three months. They say that's a right salty trail and as you well know, there can be trouble around every bend."

"Well, you keep your head down and mind what Rusty here," stroking the neck of the claybank stallion, "tells you. He's the best watchdog and protector you have so you mind, you hear me?"

Eli chuckled, "Be seein' you!"

IT WAS all of a day's journey from Walla Walla to the banks of the Columbia, just downstream from the confluence with the Walla Walla River and in the shadows of towering buttes cut by layers of dark basaltic rock. Early the next morning saw them lined out to take the ferry across the Columbia and when the sun hung high in the sky, the last of the wagons pulled onto the far shore to join the others. Sid started the wagon train off with the four freighters, each pulled by at least a six-up of mules, in the lead with the wagons of Moses and company bringing up the rear. Eli rode beside Sid as they talked about the journey ahead. "We'll keep to the south bank of the Yakima River, it comes from the Cascades and the road stays near on the south bank, crosses to the north bank 'fore we get to the Yakama Reservation. We follow that until we get past the reservation, then on to the Naches when we turn west into the mountains, but that'll be a week or so 'fore we get there."

The road hit a dry stretch, flatlands with sagebrush, cacti and clump grasses. The mules plodded onward, a thin dust cloud rising behind the freighters and enveloping the wagons of Moses and company. Eli and Sid were well ahead when Sid directed, "How 'bout you goin' on ahead, the river bends back toward the road and there will be good areas for a camp. Maybe you can get us some meat?"

Eli grinned, "If there's good water, should be some game animals. If I'm not in sight, I'll picket grey there where he can be seen while I'm scoutin' for game."

Sid nodded and reined his mount around to rejoin the wagons. Eli urged Rusty to a canter and the big stallion stretched out, the grey following free rein close behind. Eli knew the claybank would be chompin' at the bit to run and he gave him his head. The wagons fell behind and the horses pointed their noses into the wind, manes and tails flying, as Eli leaned low along the neck of his stallion, grinning and enjoying the run as much as the horses. When green showed ahead, he slowed the animals, sat up in his saddle and stood in his stirrups to look to the line of trees, cottonwoods, alders, willows and berry bushes abundant.

He walked the horses to the trees, saw a break and what appeared to be a clearing in the thicket, and stopped. Looking about and gauging the room needed for the nine wagons, he decided this would make a good camp, access to water and shade, ample space for all including pickets or rope corrals for the animals. He chuckled to himself and the difference with picking a site for an entire wagon train and doing the same for him and his two horses. He pushed into the trees to the clearing, preferring to have his own site away from the others and after stripping the gear from both animals, he picketed them within reach of water and grass and with the Spencer in hand, he ducked into the trees nearer the river and started his hunt.

Eli had always enjoyed moving through the forest, picking his steps, moving as silently as the wind that whispered through the big cottonwoods. He listened to the sounds of the woods, the chattering of a bushy-tailed squirrel that sat on a tall branch, scolding Eli as he moved ever so slowly. High above and beyond seeing, he heard the scream of a golden eagle, hunting for his family while a downy woodpecker beat his rapid cadence on a standing dead snag of a cottonwood.

Eli paused, slowly moving side to side to look through the trees and at water's edge, he saw movement. He waited, unconsciously holding his breath as he watched, and the slow movement of brown told of an animal. He dropped into a crouch, picking his way closer, moving into the edge of the clearing beside the back-water bend of the river, and there, standing knee deep amid the cattails and water lilies, a monster of a bull moose lazily chewed on greenery harvested from the deeper water. The look of the bull was mesmerizing, he appeared to be dozing, eyes closed, while he savored the feast, his dewlap swinging side to side as he chewed.

Eli stood beside a big cottonwood, leaned against it to steady his shot, and lifted the Spencer slowly and as silently as possible bringing it to full cock. The snap of the cocking hammer was heard by the bull; he stopped chewing, eyes wide open, ears twitching to catch any sound. Eli froze, waiting until the bull resumed his feast, and lifted the Spencer to his shoulder and took careful aim. He chose a spot just behind and below the bull's ear and took a breath, slowly letting it out as he began to squeeze the trigger. The Spencer bucked, roared, spat smoke and lead and the .52-caliber slug flew true, pene-trating the neck of the big beast and driving it to his knees, and then to crumple into a heap, with only his antlers and hump of his back showing above the water. There was no movement, and the water stilled. Eli had jacked another round into the Spencer, but it was not necessary. He exhaled, stepped away from the tree and moved closer. *Now the work begins. Maybe I shoulda waited till the others got here to help.*

———

THE WAGONS WERE MAKING camp just as Eli saddled the claybank. There were just a couple alders that sepa-rated his camp from the site of the wagons and Moses rode up as Eli stepped into the stirrup to swing aboard.

Eli turned at Moses greeting and said, "You're just in time. I've got some fresh meat yonder and could use a helping hand."

Moses twisted around to look at the wagons and back to Eli, and Eli added, "Just send Lucas or one of the others through the trees," motioning to the break in the trees that led to the river, "whenever they get the wagons settled."

Moses grinned, "I'll do that, yessuh, sho' will!" and turned back to help his wife and the others to set up camp.

Eli waded into the water to tie his riata around the base of the antlers and stepped back aboard to take a quick dally around the saddle horn. He turned Rusty away from the water and dug heels into his ribs as he encouraged, "Let's go boy, he's a load, that one is." The big horse leaned into the riata, pulling it taut and as the big stallion dug heels into the grassy bank, he pulled the monstrous beast from the water, kept pulling to bring it onto the grass. Eli reined up, loosed the riata, stepped down, and ground tied the big stallion and started work on the butchering of the moose.

He pulled and tugged until he had the beast on its back, and began work with his Bowie knife, splitting the hide from tail to tongue. He grabbed his hatchet from the saddlebags and began splitting the rib cage, chopping at the center bone. Once the chest was opened, he reached in to pull out the guts and with blood and bile up to his armpits, he stepped back as the guts spilled out behind the carcass. He walked back to water's edge and waded in to wash off the blood and more. Moses came into the clearing, looked at the remains, and stood with hands on hips, "Whooeee, that be some meat, yessuh."

Eli chuckled, came from the water and said, "Reckon

we need to cut it up and start passin' out the meat. Might have some hungry folks back there."

"Oh, we do, tha's fer certain!" answered Moses, chuckling and slipping his knife from the scabbard to join in the butchering. He stepped closer and dropped to one knee beside the carcass, but movement in the trees caught his attention and he looked up to see two Native warriors standing, watching, one with a rifle held across his chest, the other with a bow and nocked arrow that was held to one side. Both wore breechcloths, moccasins, with their long black hair in braids that hung over their shoulders, and with stoic expressions that bordered on anger.

Moses kept his eyes on the visitors as he reached toward Eli, but Eli said, "I see 'em. Just keep doin' what you're doin'."

Eli slowly stood, his knife held alongside his leg, "Greetings. Come near, we will share our meat with you." He dropped the knife and used the sign language he learned so many years ago when stationed at Fort Laramie and motioned the men to come into the clearing. Eli dropped to one knee and began cutting off a front quarter of the moose, bent it back to break the joint, and offered it to the men. The one with the bow replaced the arrow and the unstrung bow in his quiver and came close to accept the quarter. With Eli's help, he hefted the quarter to his shoulder, holding the leg portion to the front. The weight was all the young man could bear, but he struggled under it and reached his free hand forward to shake with Eli.

As he clasped the man's hand, Eli said, "I am Eli, this," motioning to Moses, "is my friend Moses. What are you called?"

The men frowned as they looked at Moses, their

attention had been mostly on Eli, and now as they were closer, they could see Moses was not like the men they had seen before. Both warriors frowned, stepped back as Moses stood, for he was a big man and stood a full head taller than either of them. When Moses wiped the blood off his hand and extended it to shake, he said, "I am Moses," his voice thundered in the deep bass tones and the warriors' eyes flared wide.

The older of the two timidly stepped closer and accepted Moses's hand, but watched as the big hands of Moses enveloped his hands completely. He looked wide-eyed up at the big man and carefully stepped back. His companion held his hand out as he struggled under the front quarter but accepted Moses's hand and shook it, glancing to see Eli grinning. The two men turned away and started for the trees and with a glance over their shoulder, disappeared into the woods. Moses laughed as he knelt to finish the butchering, glanced to Eli, "Reckon they ain't seen nobody big as me, 'fore."

Eli chuckled, "No, s'pose not."

# CHAPTER 15

## ONEONTA

The chug of the engine and the splash of the water as the side-wheeler *Oneonta* churned through the waters accompanied by the singing of the two colored deckhands that sang together while they worked. One was at the prow sounding for depth and the other stacked the cordwood for the boiler. Jubal and Joshua sat on the far side of the wood stack, taking their lunch break and enjoying the leftovers from the cookhouse.

"Cap McNulty said we'd be gettin' to the Cascades 'bout dark. You still think we oughta do like he said, you know, catch the *Hunt* an' go on to Portland?" asked Joshua, busy at the thick slice of roast beef he folded into the slice of bread.

"Ummhmm. Cap said he was great friends with Captain Wolf of the *Wilson G. Hunt*, and he said both boats are owned by the same company, The Oregon Steam Navigation Company. So, if we do that, Cap McNulty said he'd put in a good word for us. Then we can go on to Portland or Vancouver, but I've also been thinkin' 'bout sumpin' else," answered Jubal, cocking his head to the side to look at his brother.

Joshua frowned, familiar with the many schemes that his brother was known to hatch. "What's goin' on in that head o' yourn, now, brother?"

"If'n we don't do so good at Portland or Vancouver or some'ers else, I was thinkin' we could go on down to the mouth of the Columbia or thereabouts, and maybe sign on with a schooner or..." he shrugged, ducking his head to avoid the stern look of his brother.

"I thought you said you never wanted to go to sea like our Pa did?" asked Joshua.

"Wal, yeah, but that was just 'cuz he done it. We don't have to do like he did, you know, he went on a ship where the cap'n and crew all knew he was the son of the shipbuilder. They won't know we were ever connected with the McCains. And 'sides, it's not that different than bein' on these steamboats," offered Jubal, looking side-long at his brother.

"Other'n once we're at sea, we won't have stops ever' night so we can go ashore. And what happens if we get seasick?"

"Ah, that don't last long, once you get your sea legs. But just like this, we'd make money, don't have to worry 'bout fixin' our supper ever' night, we'd sleep in the same bunks, and see the world!" he laughed as he waved his free arm about.

"One thing for sure, we wouldn't have to be hidin' out from Pa!" declared Joshua.

"We don't hafta decide now, 'sides, we might find a grand opportunity at one o' them towns where we can make lotsa money and live high off the hog!" laughed Jubal, gobbling the last of his lunch down. He lowered his voice, "Here comes the mate, we need to get back to work."

————

THEY BROKE camp at first light and the teamsters cracked the whips over the heads of the six-up of mules to stretch out and move the heavy wagons. Sid motioned to Eli and the two took the lead, Eli trailing his grey packhorse as their horses stepped out at their own pace, distancing themselves from the wagons. The sun was just showing itself over the eastern horizon and long lances of gold tinted the sagebrush and bunchgrass of the hills on their left, painting the leaves of the scattered cottonwoods that marked the Yakima River below them on their right. They rode in silence, enjoying the country-side and the coming awake of the wilderness as long-eared jackrabbits stood erect, front paws held at their chest as they watched these strange creatures pass, but the sudden charge of a bushy-tailed coyote forced the rabbits into their holes and the disappointed coyote turned his attention to some prairie dogs standing beside their holes, soaking up the first warm rays of sunshine. The sudden whistle of the lookout sent the prairie dogs scurrying for their holes and the coyote was once again disappointed.

Sid turned to look back at the wagons, satisfied they were far enough ahead and looked to Eli, "I need to tell you something, but it's gonna take some tellin' so..."

Eli chuckled, "Take all the time you need," he slipped his pocket watch from its pocket and snapped open the lid, began to wind it and looked back at Sid, grinned, "I don't have anything else on the schedule, so, fire away!"

Sid laughed, nodded, "You were in the Union Army, right?"

"Yeah, mustered out after Appomattox."

"Ever hear of a general name of Pickett?"

"I did, I think he was famous for what became known as Pickett's Charge at Gettysburg."

"That's the one," continued Sid, "after the war was over, he was last heard of somewhere in Canada. Before he went to the war, he served in Fort Bellingham, then resigned to join the Confederates," he looked at Eli, saw him nod his understanding, and continued, "there were others that followed him, some that stayed behind, but all were Southern sympathizers. Some of 'em seized a schooner, the *J. M. Chapman*, to put to sea as a Confederate privateer."

"But the war's over, so what does that have to do with us?" asked Eli, frowning and growing impatient. It was hard enough for him to put the war behind him without others always bringing it back to the fore. He shook his head but kept his eye on the trail and listened.

"That's just it. There are still some here in the Northwest that didn't get to fight and think they need to keep it going. I think they're just tryin' to justify their outlawry, but they're still dangerous and some think Pickett might come lead 'em. Now," he paused as he looked at Eli, "this is something you have to keep under your hat, if you know what I mean?"

"I understand," answered Eli, looking at Sid with a wrinkled brow, wondering where he was going with this roundabout explanation.

"As you know, this shipment came from Bear Gulch, Hellgate, and Missoula Mills."

"Yeah, so?"

"There's more'n flour in those wagons. In the

bottoms, there is over one hundred thousand dollars in gold, placer gold mostly, 'cuz there's no mill for 'em and it's to go to Fort Steilacoom. But, if the rebels get wind of it somehow, they might try to hit us, prob'ly on the trail over Naches Pass. I put out the word we were going over Snoqualmie, not Naches, and I'm hopin' that any interested parties will look there, but…" he shrugged.

"How would anyone know about it?" asked Eli.

"There's Confederates anywhere you find more'n ten men. You've heard of Confederate Gulch on the other side of Last Chance? That's nuthin' but Southerners, and I'm sure there's some up Bear Gulch, prob'ly know there's a shipment goin' out. We tried to put the word out that the shipment went to Deer Lodge and over to Helena to go to Fort Benton, but, who knows what they'll believe?"

"Alright. Now I'm thinkin' you told me that for a reason. What'chu got on your mind?" asked Eli.

"Once we get to the mountains, I want you further ahead, far enough that if anybody's watchin' they won't think we're together. I need you to scout things out, maybe find them before they find us, and if they hit us, you can provide some additional cover behind 'em."

Eli slowly nodded, thinking about what Sid was planning, and began to question him. "What about the wagons of Moses and company, you gonna tell them?"

"Don't really want to, but what do you think?"

"You don't need to get real specific, but maybe if you tell him there might be some rebels that want what we've got and might try to take it, then he can decide if he wants to put their families in danger. But I think they deserve to make that decision themselves."

"Well, I was glad to have the extra guns, but I see what you mean, don't want to put the women and kids in danger," replied Sid. He grinned as he thought, "Maybe they'll see some land this side o' the mountains that they want to settle on!"

Eli grinned, "Maybe."

"Would you tell him? He is *your* friend," suggested Sid.

Eli chuckled, "Sure. It'll be a couple days 'fore we get to the mountains anyway, and that'll give him some time to think about it. By the way, he was askin' 'bout tomorrow, you know, it bein' Sunday an' all."

Sid frowned, "What's that got to do with anything?"

"The Lord's Day, I think they'd like to take the day off, have church services, rest up, you know, like folks do on Sundays?"

Sid shook his head, "Alright, alright. Reckon it won't hurt nuthin'."

# CHAPTER 16

## REST

"That's called Ahtanum Ridge," declared Sid, pointing to the northwest, "that marks the north boundary of the Yakama Reservation." He turned and pointed more to the north at a long ridge to the east of the river, "And that's the north end of the Rattlesnake Hills. There's a gap yonder," pointing directly ahead of their road of travel, "where the river cuts through, and the road sides it. We'll camp just this side of the cut, plenty of trees and such."

Eli nodded his understanding and pointed with his chin to their left, "There's some more of those Natives followin' us."

"Dunno what that's all about. I've been through here a time or two, never had 'em do that before. I'm hopin' there ain't no trouble brewin'. When they had that war 'afore, it was a doozy! That was 'bout eight, ten, year ago," explained Sid.

"I remember, I was still at Fort Laramie at the time, but we had our own troubles with the Sioux, Crow, Arapaho and Cheyenne. All the fightin' was about the same thing, white men encroaching on Native territory, digging for gold, killin' the buffalo," surmised Eli.

The wagon train had been traveling alongside the Yakima River for most of four days and it had been a peaceful and basically trouble-free journey, save for the usual difficulties with teams, wagons, and a few near skirmishes between the teamsters and the settlers with Moses. One of the teamsters, a displaced Southerner, Heck Philpot, had tried to stir up trouble with the coloreds, accusing them of moving too slow and costing the freighters time. But when Moses stood before the braggart and insisted he curb his language and behavior around the women and children, Philpot tried to start a fight but was handily and physically put in his place by the more experienced and capable sergeant major with no more than three punches that rocked the man back on his rear and found himself covered with dust. He spat and sputtered, grumbled and griped, but when he came to his feet, he shook his head, spat out a tooth, and returned to the campfire of the teamsters.

Moses started to apologize to Sid and Eli, but Sid stopped him with, "You didn't start it, Philpot did that all on his own. There's always got to be one that tries to be the big man in camp, and you taught him different in no uncertain terms. If anything, I should be thankin' you for not hurtin' him worse than you did. I need every man and can't spare even one." That confrontation was the day before and nothing had happened since.

Eli thought about the scuffle and looked at Sid, "By the way, Sid. You think that Philpot might be the one that was passing word to the rebel renegades about the wagon train?"

Sid frowned, "I don't think so. He's been with me since before the war was over, but he never hesitated to let others know he was a Southerner. And he's not the only one, there's at least two others, both wore grey, Amos Acker and Percival Browning. They haven't been trouble, like Philpot, but if there were a problem, they'd side him, I'm sure."

"That's good to know," replied Eli, nodding to the trees and the cut between the ridges, "That where you wanna camp?"

"Yeah, that'd be the place. Good ground, looks like there's still some graze for the animals, and there's trees for cover and windbreak." He twisted in his saddle to look at the wagons behind them, turned back to Eli, "You go ahead and find your spot, I'll direct the wagons into camp."

It was a little earlier than usual to make camp, but Sid remembered the request of Eli and the others for a day of rest and time for church. The river would also provide fish for a change for their camp cook, and the women of the wagons would appreciate a time of washing and refreshing. Sid had made the usual camp arrangements with the teamsters making their four wagons the upper end of camp and the men having two cookfires. They had chosen two of their own for cooks and divided themselves into two groups around the fires. The other wagons each had their own cookfire for the family and the men provided game to supplement what was provided by Eli and Sid.

As the lowering sun began stretching the shadows from the Ahtanum Ridge and the tall cottonwoods gathered the shadows below them, a greeting came from the dim light near the road. "Aho, the camp!" the voice came from the dark shadows of three mounted men and Eli walked from the camp to greet the visitors. He stood with a rifle cradled in his arms as he saw the figures in the dim light of the campfires, and answered, "Ho, your-self. What'chu need?"

The riders came closer, and Eli saw they were Natives, and none showed weapons but one man in the lead held one hand high, palm forward and open, as he spoke. "We are Yakama. Do you have a missionary with you?"

Eli felt the presence of someone behind him, but kept his eyes on the Natives, and answered, "A missionary? No, we do not have a missionary. Why do you ask?"

"Tomorrow is the holy day," stated the man, looking beyond Eli to the man behind him.

Moses responded, "Yes, tomorrow is the holy day we call Sunday. We will have church tomorrow. Would you like to join us for services?"

The leader smiled and nodded, turning to look back at his companions who had a similar response. "We had a man of God with us for many moons, but he had to leave. We want to hear more about the God of your people." As the man spoke, he began to frown as he looked at Moses, "But you are not a missionary, or a white man, you are a buffalo man."

Moses knew the name given to soldiers of color, and smiled and said, "Yes, but I am a man of God, and I will share from His Word in the mawnin'." He looked at the men, glanced to Eli, and looked back at the Natives, "My woman is fixin' us a meal. Would you join us?"

The Natives looked to one another, back to Moses, and the speaker nodded, "Yes. It would be good for us to eat together."

———

"WHEN WE WERE BUT BOYS, we went with our fathers to the Whitman Mission and learned about the God of the white men. But his mission was to the Nez Perce and the Cayuse people, but our people wanted to learn and we," he motioned to the other two men, "were sent to learn the ways of the white man and about their God."

Moses and his wife had learned from the three that they all carried the names of their fathers, Owhi, Meninock, and Tuckquille and each one said they had accepted Christ and wanted to worship the Lord together. Moses's wife, Ethel, asked, "Will you bring your families?"

Owhi nodded, "We will bring others also, if it is acceptable."

"Of course," answered Moses. "We will welcome all your people." He pointed to the clearing between the road and the wagons. "We will meet together there. You might want to bring blankets to sit on."

"Are there no white men that come to your church?" asked Meninock, frowning.

Moses grinned, "We've only been with these men long enough for this to be our first church service. I hope they will join us, but..." He shrugged.

The three men visited a while longer, thanked them for the meal, and rose to leave. Eli came near and expressed his thanks to the men for coming to the camp, and added, "We'll look forward to meeting more of your people."

Tuckquille was the first to shake hands with Eli, glanced to Moses, and said, "We will be here early."

Moses chuckled, "Uh, not too early. We'll have things to do first, but you'll be welcome whenever you come."

Eli frowned, for he had noticed that Moses seemed to

have lost his Southern dialect and spoke quite clearly to the Natives. He glanced to Ethel and his son, Lucas, both were smiling and knew Eli had caught on to Moses's way of talking without the usual cottonfield slang of the uneducated coloreds. Ethel leaned close to Eli, "He really is a well-read man, but he uses the slang to not sound so uppity with others."

Eli chuckled, slowly shaking his head, "And I thought I knew him better than that."

————

As THE SUN chinned itself on the eastern hills, the Native entourage was nearing the encampment of the freighters and the settlers. Moses and company were excited about the coming of the Natives and had risen early to have their morning meal and begin preparing the makings for the service and time after. The men had arranged several wooden boxes and crates for a bit of a platform for Moses so he could be seen by everyone and one of the men had a concertina and one a fiddle. They were readying to provide some music as the families from the wagons began to assemble and the Natives came near and were made welcome.

# Chapter 17

## Visitors

E li walked with Sid as they moved among the freighter wagons and Eli invited each of the men to come to the church service. One of the men asked, "Who's doin' the preachin'?"

Eli responded, "I believe Sergeant Major Moses Carpenter will be doin' the speakin'. But there will be singing and all that as well. You're all invited."

The questioner was Amos Acker, who Sid had said was one of the Southerners. He nodded his head, looked to his friend, Percival Browning, and said, "Wanna go?"

"Why not? I've heard one o' them coloreds preach afore, an' they git with it!" he chuckled.

Eli noticed the bigger man, Heck Philpot, grumble and turn away with a, "I ain't listenin' to no uppity slave preachin' to me!"

Several of the other men, some out of curiosity, some from genuine interest, chose to join with the others and go with Eli and Sid to the services. Walking from the freighters, the men noticed the number of Natives that had come from the reservation and were gathering before the makeshift platform as Moses and his wife were moving among them, greeting them and making each one welcome. Eli chuckled as he thought of the many different services he had attended both during the war and afterwards and knew this had to be one of the most unique, but he was looking forward to hearing the message from his former sergeant major. He had been an exceptional soldier, and Eli suspected he would be an even better preacher.

Moses made his way to the front of the crowd, stepped up on the makeshift platform, and lifted his hands high, "Let us ask the Lord's blessing on our service." He lowered his hands, bowed his head and dropped to one knee, holding his head with one hand and began to pray, "Our great and almighty Heavenly Father, we ask your guidance, presence and blessing on this service today. We come to you Lawd with heavy hearts, needing you to smile down upon us. We are many and different, but one under your Heaven. Lead us, guide us, and touch every heart here this mawnin'. In the mighty name of our Lawd an' Savior, Jesus, we pray!" He stood, hands uplifted, and said, "Eve'body say Amen!" and the group spoke together, and said, "Amen."

Moses looked at the crowd, frowning, "Le's try that agin! Eve'body say," he paused for just a moment, raised his voice, "Amen!" he shouted! And the entire crowd echoed this example and shouted together, "AMEN!"

Eli looked to Sid, chuckling and shaking his head, and turned back to face Moses. The big man showed a broad grin, turned to the musicians, and said, "Le's have some music!" Eli saw the fiddle player and the concertina but was surprised to see a matronly white-haired woman he had not seen before, sit down and lift a mouth harp to her lips and with a nod to each other, they began to play

"Bosom of Abraham," and with the first chord, the families of the wagons began to sing.

> *Rock o' my soul in de bosom of Abraham*
> *Rock o' my soul in de bosom of Abraham*
> *Rock o' my soul in de bosom of Abraham*
> *Lord, Rock o' my soul.*

After the families sang it through one time, Moses lifted his hands and called to the others, "Y'all heard it now, sing it with us, an' don't be quiet 'bout it!" he chuckled, winked to the three musicians, and they began to play and sing again, and the teamsters and many of the Natives lifted their voices together with the families.

After a very brief pause, and at the motion from Moses, the musicians started with another song, "Going to Shout All Over God's Heaven."

> *I've got a robe, you've got a robe*
> *All God's chillun gotta robe*
> *When I get to Heav'n, gonna put on muh robe*
> *Gonna shout all ober God's Heav'n.*
> *Heav'n, Heav'n, Ever'body talkin' 'bout Heav'n*
> *    ain't goin' there*
> *Heav'n, Heav'n, Gonna shout all ober God's*
> *    Heav'n.*

Eli and most others were enjoying the playing of the musicians as well as the singing. Eli grinned as he watched the old woman stomping her foot in time with the music and blowing into the mouth harp for all she was worth, her eyes dancing and smiling all the while. Everyone continued to sing and added verses about a crown, shoes, harp, and a song and finished with another round of the verse. This was followed by another song with a slower tempo, "Steal Away, Steal Away," which appeared to give the musicians a moment's pause, but they slowly and reverently began to play, Moses leading everyone in the singing. His deep bass voice resonating across the prairie and thrilling everyone as they joined in the heartfelt music.

> *Steal away, steal away, steal away to Jesus.*
> *Steal away, steal away home, I hain't got long to*
> *    stay here.*
> *My Lord calls me, He calls me by the thunder;*
> *The trumpet sounds it in my soul, I hain't got long*
> *    to stay here.*
> *Green trees are bending, poor sinners stand*
> *    tremblin',*
> *The trumpet sounds it in my soul, I hain't got long*
> *    to stay here.*
> *Tombstones are bursting, poor sinners stand*
> *    tremblin'*
> *The trumpet sounds it in my soul, I hain't got long*
> *    to stay here.*

It appeared that everyone enjoyed the music and Moses stood before them, lifted his hands, and began, "This mawnin' I'se gonna take muh message from the book of Proverbs, chapter 3, verses 5 and 6, *Trust in the Lord with all thine heart; and lean not unto thine own understanding. In all thy ways acknowledge Him, and He shall direct thy paths.*"

Moses held the Bible cradled in his big hand as he looked at the crowd, his penetrating gaze taking in everyone and feeling like he was peering into their very soul. The crowd stilled, no one moved as he glanced at the Bible and back to the crowd. "I want us to think of four of these words especially: trust, understand, acknowledge, and direct. Now, I have a question for you...do you trust in the Lord? I don't mean do you think about Him, or believe Him, but do you trust?"

Moses continued to expound on trusting—meaning to put all your confidence and belief in Him, and not just when you understand, but even when you don't know the end from the beginning. He spoke about acknowledge and how it was to give all the credit and honor to Him and let Him tell you where and when to go and do anything and everything. He began to close with a return to trust, "Now I'm askin', do you really trust God? Or are you trusting yourself, and I mean about gettin' to Heaven, do you really think you can get there by doing good deeds or by yourself? Nooo, you cannot. There is only one way, and that way is Jesus. Have you put your trust in Jesus? Have you accepted Him as your Savior and the only way to get to Heaven? If you're trusting anything or anyone else, you ain't gettin' there!"

He leaned forward, his gaze taking in every man, woman, and child, shook his head and stepped to the edge of the platform and stepped toward the crowd, "Now, I'm asking you," looking from one to the other, looking into their eyes and seeing each reaction, "to make that step and trust Him today, and here's how you do it, you admit you're a sinner, and know that sin has a penalty, and that penalty is death and hell forever, and you trust Jesus instead of yourself. Here's how, believe in your heart that Jesus died for you and paid for your sins and ask Him to forgive you and save you from that eternal hell!" His deep voice rolled like thunder and Eli looked about, watching the response of so many that had their heads bowed and were listening intently to every word of the preacher.

Moses continued, "Now, if you want to trust Him with all your heart and are willing to repent of your sins, then say a simple prayer like this—Dear God," and he paused between each passage, "I want to trust you today —to take me to Heaven when I die—forgive me of my sins—and give me that gift of eternal life. Thank you for that gift. In Jesus' name I pray, Amen."

There was a low murmur from many in the crowd as they repeated the prayer and the Amen with Moses. For a moment, no one moved, no one spoke, all looked to the big man whose heart had been stirred. He lifted his hands and face to Heaven, and shouted, "AMEN! THANK YOU, JESUS!" And his words were echoed by a jubilant crowd. He looked to the crowd, a deep rumble of rejoicing seemed to come from deep within, and his bass voice repeated, "Thank you, Jesus, thank you." He looked to the crowd, "Now, everyone is invited to join the families of the wagons behind me and partake of the feast our ladies have prepared for everyone!"

The Natives looked to one another and when the three men that had come the night before turned to them, they spoke among themselves, and happy faces reflected their willingness to stay and eat with the families. Eli looked at the teamsters who were anything but hesitant, for they had already tired of eating their own cooking and the thought of a woman-cooked meal did not need a second invitation.

Sid and Eli followed the others and entered the semicircle of the wagons and were surprised to see the many tables set up and loaded with an assortment of food-stuffs, including pies made from the abundance of berries that grew near the river. The sharing of food and the time together did much to still the troubled waters between the settlers and the teamsters. The Natives showed their appreciation and thanks as they talked with the families. Even the children were seen playing together. Eli smiled, thinking how such a simple thing as singing and sharing did so much to bridge gaps between peoples.

# CHAPTER 18

# SEPARATION

Eli had made his usual trek to the top of the hill behind his camp for his early morning time in prayer and reading the Bible and spent some time making his visual survey of the land and the trail with his binoculars. Satisfied there were no immediate threats or dangers, he walked down the long slope, the slow-rising sun beginning to paint the mountains with shades of pale pink as it stretched the shadows of the cottonwoods at the edge of his camp.

He sensed, rather than saw, someone in his camp. With his rifle cradled in his arms across his chest, he stealthily pushed through the brush and spotted the big figure of Moses sitting beside the little cookfire. He had taken the liberty of preparing a pot of coffee that danced on the rock while the flames licked at its side, cups sat near to take the morning chill off the metal. His back was to Eli, but his deep voice greeted, "Coffee's 'bout ready, Colonel."

Eli chuckled as he stepped from the trees, "A man

could get spoiled with treatment like that, Sergeant Major."

"Oh, I ain't 'bout to spoil you, suh. That's as much for me as it is you," he chuckled, the laughter shaking his frame as his eyes danced with mischief.

Eli leaned his rifle against the log, sat his possibles pouch down beside it and stretched, arched his back, and sat down to reach for the pot and pour himself a cup of the welcome eye-opener. He looked over at Moses, saw a somber expression on the usually smiling face, and asked, "So, what do I owe this visit to? I thought you'd be gettin' your folks ready to move out. Sid is wanting to get an early start this morning."

"That's just it, Colonel. Ya' see, after we had church and lunch yestiddy, we had us a long visit with many o' them Yakama folks. An' those three, Owhi, Meninock, and Tuckquille, they're leaders of their people, an' we went for a ride with 'em, they showed us some land on th'other side o' the river, yonder," pointing to the east side of the Yakima River, "and we seen us some fine land. They said their land was on the west side o' the river, and they was ranches up north and places, but the land yonder, well, it's open!" He reached for his cup, took a long sip, and lifted his eyes to Eli, "Ya' see, Colonel, they wants us'ns to stay 'roun 'chere. They wanna have church wit' us, be neighbors. They wan' us to teach 'em 'bout farmin' and such, they'll teach us 'bout this land and more."

He took a deep breath that lifted his shoulders, took another draught of coffee, and looked at Eli, let a slow smile split his face, "Suh, we ain't never been welcomed like this afore, these are good folks!" He chuckled, looked at Eli, and added, "I think we done found us a home!"

Eli grinned, "I'm happy for you, Moses. You and your people deserve to have a good home, family, neighbors, and more. Yessir, I'm happy for you." He paused, looking at his friend, "But don't get the wrong idea, you'll be missed, and I'll be back ever' now'n then to check on you, but I am happy for you."

"I thot that's what you'd say, but I knows we tol' Mistuh Six that we'd be goin' o'er the mountains wit' him, but...well, would you tell him?"

"Don't you concern yourself with that, Moses. He'll understand." He glanced around, back to Moses, stood, "But I'm gonna hafta break camp."

Moses stood, and said, "Yessuh, but you'll stop to say g'bye to the missus?"

"I will, Moses, I will."

———

ELI HAD DISAPPEARED through the gap carved by the Yakima River that split the long ridges to the east and west by the time the four freighters were ready to stretch out. Sid had sent the mule wrangler with the cavvy of extra mules ahead when the first wagon driven by Heck Philpot started to move. He cracked his long bullwhip over the heads of the eight mules, shouted at them and they leaned into their collars, pulled the trace chains taut and the wagon rocked off its tracks and began to move. His was the heaviest wagon and led the way with eight mules in harness. Three wagons followed, each with six mules, and with the settler families of the wagon train standing and waving, the four freighters crawled through the gap, the road on the narrow shoulder above the river. By midmorning they were crossing the Naches River about three miles upstream of the confluence with the

Yakima at a cut at the northwest end of the Yakima Ridge. The Naches Trail would follow the river into the mountains and beyond.

Sid had asked Eli to stay well ahead of the wagons, scouting for any sign of a rebel renegade attack. He had crossed the Naches just as the sun was full and warming his back and followed the old Indian trail that had been put to use as a wagon route to cross over the Cascades. The Naches Valley was a long, fertile green valley that stretched from the southeast to the northwest for about fifteen miles. Low foothills framed the valley, rising above with the sagebrush crested hills that eons ago had been washed from the high mountains by violent thunderstorms. The Creator had carved them with His fingertips to prepare them for the many Native peoples that would make it their home.

Time and again, Eli watched pronghorn, mule deer, and elk that lazily grazed on the tall grasses of the valley. On the far side of the river, he saw the roofs of a home, barns, and more, where one of the early settlers established his home and ranch to raise cattle for settlers and gold seekers. He knew there were a few ranches in these fertile valleys, but he also knew it would be decades before this country would see the settlement like those further east.

The hills began to crowd together, the long butte on the south side of the river with its long line of basaltic rimrock that hung threateningly over the talus slopes, hovered over the river, while on the north, taller rocky hills stood tall, broad shoulders rising above the green valley, dark shadows filling the ravines as the sun began to lower beyond the taller mountains upstream. Eli spotted a young buck, strips of velvet hanging from his antlers, come from the river, pause, and look at the intruder. Eli slipped the Winchester from the scabbard, jacked a round in the chamber causing the buck to start away, but Eli lifted the rifle and snapped off a shot that took the buck just behind his front shoulder and driving him to the ground in a heap. *That'll be supper and some work to smoke it out 'fore I leave in the mornin'.*

The river hugged the butte on his left, but the cottonwoods and alders hid the water yet also offered a campsite. He dropped to the ground beside the buck, ground tied the horses, and began to field dress the deer. Once the buck was gutted, he lifted the carcass, minus the head and legs, to the top of the packs on the grey, then led both horses into the trees for their camp. His usual routine, stripping the gear from the horses, stacking the packs and saddles, giving the horses a rubdown, and giving them a drink and a time to roll, took little time as was his habit. With a small fire going, coffee heating, he hung the carcass from a big limb and began skinning it out and cutting some steaks for his supper.

A stomping and snort from the big stallion turned Eli away from the carcass to search the trees for whatever had alarmed the claybank. He looked at Rusty, saw his ears pricked, nostrils flaring, and head lifted as he pawed at the dirt. Something was alarming the big horse, and Eli reached for his rifle as he searched the trees. A flash of black fur dropped him to one knee to look below the branches for a better look. His first thought was wolf, and where there was one, there were more. The scent of the fresh kill had been the attraction, but he had left the gut pile and bones at least a hundred yards from his camp. He had seen the turkey buzzards, ravens, magpies, and even an eagle drop to the carrion, but the only other predators had been a couple coyotes, a badger, a bobcat, and a covey of crows.

He searched the trees, saw movement but not enough for a shot, watched carefully and listened, expecting an attack, or an attempt to get to the hanging meat that was behind him. Rusty did a quick sidestep and snorted as he turned to look behind Eli, but the flash of black snatched a cast-off scrap and disappeared into the trees before Eli could turn. But something about the meat thief bothered Eli, it wasn't big enough for a wolf, too big for a raccoon, too bold for a coyote, but what was it? Eli stood and moved to Rusty's side, using his left hand to stroke the neck of the horse, spoke softly so both horses could hear, and waited for another sneak attack from the canine. But nothing came, nothing moved, and the horses relaxed and returned to their grazing.

Eli shook his head, gave the trees another look through, and returned to the task of butchering the buck. With four backstrap steaks in hand, he went to the fire and hung them over the flames with long willow withes anchored in the dirt. He retrieved a couple potatoes from the panniers and went to river's edge to coat them in mud, packed them like a snowball, and returned to the fire to bury them in the hot coals.

While he waited for his dinner, he returned to his butchering and deboning the meat. It was just a short while until he had the meat stacked on a part of the hide near the big rock at fire's edge. He would cut it into thin strips and put them on the willow smoking rack, but that would wait until after supper. He poured himself a cup of coffee, reached for a willow stick with a steak and paused, frowning. *Wait a minute! I put four steaks out to broil, now where's the other one!*

He looked about, and at the edge of the fire, paw prints showed clearly in the moist dirt that he had scraped aside for his fire. The prints were too small for a wolf, but too broad for a coyote whose prints are more of an oval while these were broader, like a wolf, but small. He frowned as he looked around the camp, searching the trees, and began to think it might be a wolf, but a small one, maybe an orphaned pup. He looked at the horses; although watchful, they were not alarmed.

He finished his supper, sipped his coffee, and thought about his visitor. He grinned mischievously and rose to start preparing for the smoking of the meat. He gathered an armful of willows, cut and tied them to make his rack, and cut the meat into thin slices and strips. With shovel in hand, he scooped coals from the fire and lay a bed for the coals, placed the rack over the coals, and began laying the strips of meat on the willows. Once the rack was full, he placed alder branches over the coals and the smoke began to rise. He would have to tend the rack often, but it would be well worth it to have a parfleche full of smoked meat. But he was also thinking about the black meat thief and gathered some of the scraps and placed them about, all within sight, and with a fresh cup of coffee, began his vigil.

Full dark had fallen, and the only light was the shafts of moonlight that pierced the cover of leaves, when Eli saw Rusty lift his head quickly and look toward him and beyond. Although the horse watched, he was not alarmed, and Eli knew whatever he saw was not a threat. Eli slowly turned his head and looked to see an emaciated wolf pup, ribs showing, skinny legs trembling, as he gobbled down one of the scraps. Eli tossed another scrap toward him, and he jumped back, but did not leave. With a quick look at Eli, the pup dropped and crawled toward the new offering and snatched it up and gobbled it down. Eli tossed another, closer, and the pup repeated his actions, but after devouring the tidbit, he dropped to his belly and stretched out, looking at Eli, cocking his head side to side, anticipating another offering. He was not disappointed.

Eli waited, did not throw any more meat, but began to talk low and slow, trying to establish trust. He did not move, but neither did the pup. Eli glanced to the horses, saw Rusty and Grey had turned away, no longer interested in the furry visitor but more interested in the grass at their feet. Eli slowly rose, went to the smoker and with the shovel put the last of the coals on the alder wood, and decided to go to his blankets. The pup had trotted to the trees with a full belly that should make him sleepy. Eli searched the trees for him, but he was not to be seen. Eli grinned, rolled out his blankets, and turned in for the night.

# CHAPTER 19

## COMPANY

Something woke Eli but his first glance to the horses showed no alarm, both were standing hipshot, heads down, sleeping. He did not move anything but his eyes, then slowly reached under the blanket to grasp the butt of his Colt. He listened to the sounds of the night, the distant chuckle of the river as it bounced over the rocks, the trill of a red-winged blackbird looking for a mate, and the cry and bark of a pair of coyotes, but there were no howls of wolves. He looked to the stars in a sky unmarred by clouds and watched the slow dance of the treetops, but nothing was out of the ordinary nor alarming. He frowned, trying to remember what had brought him awake when something stirred at his back. He froze, not breathing, just listening and the whisper of movement behind him warned him but he slowly moved only his hand and arm under the blankets as he cautiously rolled to his back, pistol in hand, only to see a dark shadow on the ground, unmoving except for eyes that reflected orange and turned his direction.

The wolf pup had come to his side, seeking company,

warmth, security, and food. Eli knew wolves were pack animals and from birth were always in the company of others, even though the pack was ruled by the strongest male with his primary mate at his side. He also knew there were pack leaders that were threatened by any other male, even his own pups, and would chase them from the pack, keeping only his primary mate and her offspring of females. Perhaps that is what happened to this pup, or his mother could have been killed or injured rendering her unable to feed her litter.

Whatever the mystery, he knew he would never know, but his concern now was what to do with the addition to his pack. Eli rolled back to his side, slipped the Colt back into the holster, and felt the pup move even closer. Eli breathed deeply, burrowed into his blankets, and decided to take it one day at a time.

When the night sky was just beginning to snuff out its lanterns and shed its darkness, Eli looked about, turned to see the pup had gone, and came from his blankets. He stood, stretched, and walked closer to the smoke rack, saw nothing had been touched and with a shrug he stirred up the coals, added some wood, and with coffeepot in hand went to the river's edge for fresh water.

With the coffeepot on the rock beside the cookfire, Eli took his Bible, binoculars, and Winchester and climbed the hill behind him for his typical survey of the trail and time with his Lord. He greeted the beginning of the day as the first color made the eastern sky blush in pink and after his time in prayer, he read a few passages in the scriptures then with binoculars in hand, he began his survey of the trail before him.

There were deer coming down to water, a small bunch of elk came from a narrow valley and creek that fed the Naches from the south, and he saw upstream about two to three miles where the river bent to the north around a shoulder of the north hills. He searched the brush, trees and more, and realized he was looking for the wolf pup. He chuckled to himself, shook his head, put the binoculars back in the case, and started back to camp.

He examined the smoked meat, checked several pieces, and decided the meat needed more smoking to be cured. He put more coals on the bed, added alder branches, and used his ground cover to lay over the rack to keep the smoke on the meat longer. He nodded his satisfaction with his handiwork and returned to the fire for his coffee. He added the ground coffee to the pot, moved it closer to the fire, and cut off a couple steaks from the backstrap of the deer, meat he was saving to broil for his meals, rather than smoking to cure.

When the coffee was ready, he added a little cold water to settle the grounds, poured himself a cup and sat back to wait for the steaks to broil. He thought about the day before him, thinking he would probably be on the trail for a couple days before nearing the area where Sid had explained would probably be the terrain where any attack might come. From what he had seen so far, the road was out in the open and he would be exposed to any attack, a thought that did not sit well with Eli. His way was to usually keep to the trees, find a game trail or ancient trail of the Natives, and stay out of sight. He hoped that he would find that kind of trail further along and well before any possible attack, but he would have to do what he had become accustomed to while commanding the cavalry unit in the war, adapt. Whatever was thrown your way, adapt, always adapt.

He reached for the willow that held his steak and

noticed he had a visitor. On the far side of the fire, the black wolf had come into camp and bellied down without Eli seeing him. Eli grinned, reached to the ground between his feet and grabbed a scrap of meat and tossed it to the furry canine. The pup caught the morsel with little movement and appeared to swallow it whole. He lifted his head, mouth open, tongue lolling, waiting for more.

"What am I goin' to do with you, you little beggar?" asked Eli as he tossed another morsel.

"You probably already had your own breakfast and just came back here for more, didn't you?" questioned Eli, reaching for another tidbit. "If you think I'm gonna feed you all the time, you might go hungry!"

The pup sat up, and Eli swore he was smiling at him, as he looked with that expression with his mouth open and tongue lolling. "So, who's adopting who? You makin' yourself a part of my pack, or what?"

Eli stripped his steak off the willow and began to eat, the juices dripping down his chin and the wolf watching every bite, but Eli did not share this choice steak with his visitor. When he finished, wiped his hands of the grease, he picked up his cup and sipped some more coffee, all the while the two looked at each other. Eli stood to go to the packs and prepare to leave. When he turned back to the rack, the wolf was gone. Eli glanced around the camp, looked into the trees, but there was nothing.

With a shrug and a shake of his head, he grinned and readied the gear and packs, filling the two parfleche with the smoked meat. The sun had just lifted itself above the eastern horizon when Eli rode from the trees onto the trail and as he rode, he continued his search for the trail of the ancients, preferring the cover of the trees to the exposed clearings and flats of the road that had been cleared and made into a wagon road for settlers and freighters.

The Naches River twisted and turned its way through the basalt-covered hills that often rose two to three thousand feet higher than the river bottom, always stretching their shadows to the river and the roadway, seldom allowing the lances of sunlight to reach the bottom of the steep-sided valley. Always vigilant, missing nothing. If he had been watched one would think he never turned his head but continually stared straight ahead, but his eyes were constantly on the move, missing nothing. When a bald eagle tucked his wings and began his dive from hundreds of feet above, Eli watched, looking to the river below and knew the golden winged predator had already spotted his prey and the instant before the long talons showed themselves, he saw the flash of silver in the water that heralded the vain attempt at escape. When the big wings spread and lifted the eagle and his catch from the river, Eli nodded in approval and learned from the feathered master hunter about never exposing yourself until the last possible second.

As he watched the eagle lift, a glimpse of black told Eli of the presence of his friend, too small to be a mature wolf, but swift enough to stay with the long-legged stallion. But Eli was concerned about the wolf pup, would he have the stamina to last? But that thought was set aside when he saw a black bear sow, standing tall on her hind legs and watching as her two cubs were frolicking off the far bank of the river, right where the road crossed over and in the path of the wolf cub. *Now this will be interesting.*

Eli reined up just as Rusty and the grey were getting a little skittish, for they too had seen or smelled the family at play and had heads lifted and ears pricked as they watched. Eli sat with arms crossed on the pommel as he leaned forward to watch. He frowned when the two cubs looked like three, all rolling and tussling. He looked at the sow, who dropped to all fours and padded closer to the playing furballs. She paused, watching each one, moved closer and slapped at one who was sent rolling, looked at the others and lowered her head and nipped at the rump of another, then turned to the last one who Eli recognized as the wolf pup, and the sow cocked her head to the side, growled and snarled, reached out with one paw and slapped at the pretender, and sent him scurrying away. One of the cubs rose up and lifted his paw as if waving goodbye, then dropped to all fours and followed his mother into the trees.

Eli sat up, dug his heels into Rusty's ribs, and pushed across the shallows of the Naches River as the current splashed against the knees of the horses and nudged them on their way. When they climbed the bank, the wolf cub was sitting in the middle of the roadway, mouth open, tongue lolling, and mischief showing in his eyes. As the horses shook off the excess water, the pup took off up the trail, disappearing into the trees.

The road made a sharp bend to the north, as the hills shouldered close, and a pinnacle of basalt stood as a sentinel to guard the dogleg bend back to the west as the road hung on the steep hillside on the north. The valley had narrowed allowing only the river to pass. The trail disappeared, forcing Eli to take to the river and push the horses against the current, wading in knee-deep water on the rocky and gravelly bottom for almost a mile, until the canyon widened, and the trail showed once again. The river renewed its dance of twists and turns, causing the road to cross over time and again, until the hills pushed back and offered a grassy-bottomed valley, lush with green grass, patches of flowers, and game aplenty.

Across the river on the south side, the green hills were thick with ponderosa, fir, and spruce and beckoned Eli. He nudged Rusty into the water, trailed the grey close behind and soon found a trail that led into the trees. Although the narrow strip of trees was no more than twenty yards wide on the bottom of the hills, it was a welcome refuge and he had gone no more than a hundred yards when he spotted the black fur running through the trees, teasing his followers and daring them to follow. Eli chuckled, saw a bit of a clearing between the tree line and the river, and decided it was time for a midday break and some coffee.

As expected, the wolf cub joined them, taking his place at the edge of the trees, well away from the horses and Eli, but within throwing distance of any tasty morsel. After his coffee and midday snack of fresh smoked meat, Eli found a shady spot on the uphill side of the clearing, under the wide branches of a big ponderosa and made himself comfortable, legs stretched out, hat over his eyes, the horses grazing on the grass, and started a nap. He felt the warmth and weight of a furry head on his lap. He grinned and nodded off.

# CHAPTER 20

## HIGH COUNTRY

The narrow trail twisted through the heavy timber, packed down by the ancient peoples and the many beasts of the forests. Eli spotted scat from bears, droppings from elk, deer, even moose. There were scrapings on the trees where the antlered animals marked their passing in midsummer when they scraped the velvet from their racks. Porcupine gnawed on bark, leaving the trees scarred for life, and grizzly reached high to tell the world how big they were by digging their long claws deep in the resinous bark.

With an occasional glimpse of black fur, Eli grinned at the tenacity and vitality of the wolf pup, often seeing him lying in the trail, waiting for his adopted family, only to scamper on ahead again. The high country and thick timber offered cover and seclusion, but at each clearing when the sun offered a touch of warmth, Eli would stop, look around, and take in the beauty of the purple lupine, yellow coneflower, the reddish-purple primrose, and the deep blue larkspur. Wherever there were patches of flowers, there would usually be deadfalls from previous blowdowns or long past lightning-caused fires.

He kept to the north-facing slopes where the timber was thick but offered glimpses of the river and road below and the bald south-facing slopes on the far side of the river. He had seen sign of the previous passing of several wagons and thought he might overtake them, but they were making good time and might reach the crest long before he would. No matter, he knew not who they were but guessed they were families for he had seen tracks of women and children walking beside the wagons which was typical where there was a hard-pulling climb for the teams.

The Naches Trail, because it followed the river through the mountains and the valley, was often crowded by the steep-sided hills, forcing people to cross the river many times, sometimes even to travel in the river. Eli came to a narrowing of the valley where the basaltic cliffs and escarpments on the mountain forced even the narrow game trail to cross the river until the valley widened and the hills pushed back again. This was rugged country, hillsides were scarred by the jagged rocks, twisted pines and cedar, steep slopes that bore talus slides, often allowing little or no penetration of direct sunlight. But the trail through the trees was smooth, hard packed, and made easy by the passage of many feet. Although there were places where Eli could see no more than ten or twenty feet ahead, he trusted the way of the ancients and continued.

Eli rounded a shoulder and had a glimpse of the valley below. It widened with the slopes on the north laying back, carrying thick timber that covered the faces on long, low slopes that slowly rose to the higher hills a mile or more beyond. While the south side of the river had slow-rising hills, all were blanketed with thick black timber, with occasional draws and gullies showing the light green of aspen. The valley bottom waved with tall grasses that reminded Eli of the ocean tides, before meeting the cottonwoods, willows, and alders that lined the riverbanks.

The break in the timber afforded him a view of the valley bottom and the road, and Eli searched the valley for sign of the wagons, but nothing moved, and no white canopies of wagons showed anywhere.

The Naches Trail had lost some favor when the Snoqualmie Road was finished. But for travelers, the Naches was over a hundred miles shorter, although the road and pass were steeper and more difficult, yet many of the wagon trains of settlers preferred the easier route and had chosen to take to the Snoqualmie to cross the Cascade Mountains to get to the Puget Sound area. But Eli was never one for following the crowd and even if he was not working with Sid Six and the freighters, he would choose the Naches Trail. The trail he followed through the timber, although not allowing much direct sunlight, began to grow dark and he knew the sun was lowering and it was getting on to time to make camp. Typical of thick-timber trails, the animals that used them often broke through the trees in their search for water and graze, leaving a lesser trail for others to follow. Eli spotted such a trail and turned toward the river.

The bottom of the hill splayed out and offered a flat, grassy area sided by aspen for Eli to make camp. He could catch a glimpse of the river through the trees but stopped short and stepped down to strip the gear from the horses. He led them to the water, gave them a rubdown with a handful of grass, and led them back to the campsite, all the while thinking of his supper. He grinned as he decided he was going to have trout for supper.

With the horses picketed, gear stacked, and no sign of the wolf pup, Eli started back to the water. He had seen a bit of a cutback where the river bent away from the south hills and knew that was the place he wanted. Well back from the bank, he chose his site where the grass was thick all the way to the rounded edge of the bank. He dropped to all fours, crawled to water's edge, and bellied down, parallel to the flow of the river. He slowly reached into the water, feeling his way down the bank to the undercut caused by the current and ever so slowly, hand open but slightly cupped, he searched the undercut. When he felt the gentle movement of the back fin of a trout, he moved his hand forward against the current, lightly feeling the fins of the trout, and when his hand was in just the right place, he quickly slid his hand forward, grasped the trout, and brought it out. His fingers had slipped to where they were just inside the gills and gave him an inescapable grip. He tossed the big trout onto the grass, watched it flop, and went for another.

Focused on his fishing, he caught a glimpse of black fur slightly behind him, grinned, and kept after the fish. *I reckon three or four will be enough for both of us.* He grabbed another, tossed it with a backhand onto the grass, and searched for another. He belly crawled a little further upstream, kept his hand at the undercut, and found another big trout. This last one was the biggest and he almost lost it, but finally got it out of the water and had to rise on his knees to ensure he tossed it well away from the water, concerned it would flop back in and escape. He held it out before him, heard a grunt behind him, and over his shoulder said, "Oh go on, Lobo, you've got enough already!"

Another grunt came, followed by a low throated roar, and Eli froze in place. He thought he had smelled something different and slowly turned to see a yearling boar black bear enjoying his feast on the fish. He was sitting on his haunches, looking much like a fat-bellied man with his hind legs outstretched and holding the fish with his front paws as he tore it apart with his big teeth. Eli looked around quickly, hoping there was no mother bear with this delinquent boar and saw nothing. Eli kept his grasp on the big trout, rose slowly and in a crouch, walked away through the tall grass, the fish in one hand, his Winchester in the other, never taking his eyes off the bear.

When he walked into camp, the horses were both standing, heads high, ears pricked, nostrils flaring as they looked past Eli and through the trees behind him, undoubtedly smelling the bear and showing their concern. Eli made a last look at the bear still by the riverbank, saw him drop to all fours and pad away through the willows, probably looking for more fish. Eli shook his head, breathed deep in relief, and began gathering firewood to cook his trout. When he returned, arms full of wood, he saw the wolf pup, belly down, and watching Eli. He opened his mouth, licked his lips, and Eli glanced to the big rock where he laid his fish, and was relieved to see it was still there. He looked at the wolf, "Well Lobo, it's a good thing. If you had gotten that big trout, I'da had to skin you and have you for supper!" He realized he had used the word lobo as a name and shook his head, "Just like a woman! Here I go naming the little beggar, and then I'll get to feelin' sorry for him, and then…" he growled his disgust at himself and muttered, "just like a woman!"

He built the fire, but before he lit it, he had a whiff of smoke. He frowned, stood, and looked about, peering through the trees at every cut, looking to the road below and beyond, but dusk had lowered its curtain and he could not see much. He heard what he thought was the distant roll of thunder, but the wind was picking up and whistling through the pines and it only lasted a few moments, so he turned away. *Oh well, probably just the wagons fixin' supper. After it gets full dark, I'll have a look-see and prob'ly see their fires.* He returned to his supper fixing and started his fire, put the coffeepot close to begin boiling the water, and set about cleaning the fish.

While he ate his supper, he was certain he smelled more smoke, other than his own fire, but after his look-see, he had to shrug it off and soon turned in for the night. He made a lean-to shelter just in case the thunder turned into a rainstorm and crawled under, stretched out blankets, and snuggled down for the night. Lobo did not come close until well after he had dozed off, but Eli felt the warmth from his nearness and grinned.

# CHAPTER 21

# DEVASTATION

The morning broke clear and crisp and Eli welcomed the new day from his promontory on the point of a timbered hill about five hundred feet above his camp. He had grown uncomfortable and concerned before the first light and made his early morning jaunt by the light of the lowering moon and the last of the starlight. He had that sensation at the back of his neck that had always been a warning of impending danger and he always heeded the feeling, but this morning showed nothing alarming. The road below was empty, deer still tiptoed their way to the river for their morning water, and even Lobo had shadowed him as he climbed the hill. But now he sat, elbows on his knees, searching the trees and the trail for anything or anyone. Nothing showed, but he was unsatisfied. He glanced to the wolf and even he was standing tall, looking up the valley and beyond, head high and leaning into the breeze. A low growl came from deep within his chest, and Eli searched the hills again. Nothing. Lobo glanced to his friend, back to the high country, and followed Eli off the point to return to camp.

Eli had an early start but avoided the road and kept to the trail of the ancients that wove through the dark timber yet continued to follow the Naches River and stayed in the river canyon. The terrain varied, the hills pushed in and stood tall, then lay back and offered easy passage. The trail climbed higher, crossing over a rounded shoulder that bore the blackened timber of an old fire, and rose above a talus slope of basaltic rock. Whenever he crested or neared a promontory, Eli would step down and use his binoculars to search the road and hillsides for any possible danger and always in the back of his mind was the warning of Sid about the renegade Confederates.

The trail he followed crossed another long shoulder, dropped into a narrow valley just above the confluence of the Naches River and another that came from the west while the Naches bent around a point and continued on its northwest course. The low breeze wafted the pungent sweet scent of pines and other scents of the wild were carried on the valley winds. Eli grinned as he got a whiff of a skunk, a little later the musky stench of a bear that made the horses a little skittish, and the underlying scent of decaying leaves and wood that was always present in the hill country. He was beginning to think that the smell of smoke from the previous night had been from a campfire and had been snuffed out, until he crested another ridge, and in the distance, a thin tendril of smoke rose from the trees near the river bottom, probably another mile or two away. There was no reason to be concerned about a campfire, there was nothing unusual about that for most every traveler would stop near midday and have a meal and if they were anything like Eli, they would want some coffee. But lingering on the wind was another smell, a gut-grinding and offensive smell, the smell of burning flesh. Unlike the smell of meat cooking, burning flesh of a body had an unforgettable stench that assaulted and offended every sense of man. It wasn't strong yet, but every step seemed to bring them closer.

The trail kept to the south side of the river and Eli spotted a sharp embankment that stood about a hundred feet higher than the river bottom and held a long talus slope as the river splashed against it and was forced to make a bend to pass. Eli looked above the bench to see the taller mountains that rose at least two thousand feet higher and were scarred near the crest with an old blow-down that left brown and decaying carcasses of once tall and proud pines and spruce trees. In the river bottom, the stream cascaded over a shear drop and crashed over the rocks below, leaving behind a cascading waterfall and a long stretch of white water cascades. The water and mist that rose seemed to wash the stench from the air as Eli passed the special touch of God's creative artistry.

The narrow trail kept to the thicker trees that skirted the north-facing slopes and overlooked the river below. But the smell of smoke and burning flesh returned and Eli lifted his neckerchief to cover his mouth and nose, dreading what he was going to find. It was about a mile and a half when the trail broke from the trees, overlooked the river, and started to rise to a long ridge above the water, but that short glimpse showed Eli what he dreaded.

On the far side of the river, the remains of what had been wagons, now showed black skeletons of wagons, wheels, a few scattered remnants of belongings that had been searched, carcasses of horses and mules, and a large circle of black that Eli knew was the funeral pyre that had sent its stench downriver.

Turkey buzzards, ravens, magpies, coyotes, a badger, a bobcat, and two foxes were scrambling about, searching for any tidbits of carrion. The carcasses of the animals were covered with every manner of carrion eater, and two carcasses of women, identifiable only by the nearby dresses, were the exclusive domain of two big vultures, one with its head deep inside the rib cage of one.

Eli dropped off the trail, crossed the river, and tethered the horses. With his shovel in hand, he started toward the semicircle of burnt wagons, examining every track or sign that might have been left by the raiders. The settlers had chosen a camp on a wide bend in the river that offered a stretch of land between the road and the river with grass and scattered trees for cover. They had parked the wagons in a semicircle, with the river closing the circle, an area that would normally be an exceptional site and offering an easily defensible position. But whatever band of outlaws or renegades that had attacked, came from the uphill side beyond the road, and the shallow river below the site. Only one horse had been killed, the rest of the carcasses were mules which told Eli that these were probably white men. Most Natives would take the horses and eat the mules, but there was no sign of butchering on the mule carcasses. As he walked among the wagons, he saw where the bodies of men and boys had been thrown on the big fire, while the women and girls had been used and abused before being brutally murdered. There were none that had been scalped and no sign of the usual mutilation of hated enemies. This had not been done by Natives.

The upstream end of the isthmus had a bit of a hill with a shear drop-off and Eli chose that for the burial site. He scattered the carrion eaters, and after fetching Rusty, he dragged the bodies to the low spot, filled the depression with the bodies or remains of five women and three girls, then added the bits and pieces of charred remains and boots, shoes, and more from the funeral pyre, then climbed atop the hill and began shoveling the dirt over the remains. When he finished, he stood above the mass grave, spoke a brief prayer, and went to the river for a bath and clothes washing. He had gathered the few personal belongings that were scattered about and buried them together at the end of one of the wagons. There were bits of jewelry, a partially burned Bible, other small items. He shook his head as he covered them over thinking how little it was to tell of so many lives.

As he put the site of the massacre behind him, he lifted his face to the heavens, and said, "Lord, you know what I'm thinkin' and you know what needs to be done. If I'm to be the instrument of your vengeance, then give me the guidance, strength, and wherewithal to get the job done right. These vile vermin need to be wiped off this earth," he growled, then shook his head, put his hat back on and said, "Amen!"

He took to the tracks of the raiders, and with close examination he guessed there to be eight to ten raiders, but they were leading the horses taken from the wagons and that bunch numbered another six horses, led in a long string at the tail end of the group. They kept to the road, either because they had no fear of being caught, or they were too stupid to know better. Eli could easily see the tracks of the bunch and took to the trees, finding a game trail that held to the hillside and the trees above the road and river, and began his pursuit.

He crested a low ridge, kept to the trees but paused to look at the long, wide basin before him. He leaned on the pommel, thinking, watching, calculating. These raiders would have been lying in wait for their target, probably thinking these wagons were the ones carrying the gold. Once the attack began, the evil nature of immoral men that had become vile and vindictive, some by the depravity of war, others by the insane jealousy and lust for what others had, turned their attention to the prize at hand and yielded to their lusts. But now their thoughts would turn back to their original purpose, to take the gold that would enrich them all.

Eli believed they would return to their lair, keep watch for the coming freighters, and seek to fulfill their original plan. Their lair, now where would that be? He twisted around to retrieve his binoculars and looked to the towering spruce beside him. He stood on his saddle, reached high for a big branch, and climbed higher into the tree. Shielded from the sun by the thick branches, he had no fear of the sun reflecting on the lenses to flash his presence. He found a sturdy perch and began his scan. *Now, if I were the raiders, where would I be hiding?*

The wide basin stretched about four miles upstream of the Little Naches River, but at its widest was no more than three-quarters of a mile. Except for the twisting river in the bottom, the floor of the valley was thick with black timber, but at the end, a long-ridged hill rose at least fifteen hundred feet higher than the valley floor. Almost bald on the south-facing slope, with newer growth timber on the steeper slope facing down valley, probably due to some fire decades before, it offered a perfect promontory for a lookout to see anything and everything that came up the road from below, allowing the raiders ample time to mount an attack. As he scanned the hillside, he focused in on the valley below the peak, saw a grey rope of smoke twist above the trees, and grinned, "Gotcha!"

Eli chuckled as he mentally mapped out what would be his approach to reach the camp of the raiders for his singular attack. He looked to the lower hills closer to his position, the different ravines that carried feeder runoff creeks, and calculated his route. With another look, a closer examination of his planned route, and with a sadistic grin, he lowered himself to the saddle, replaced the binoculars, and chuckled when he saw Lobo lying in the trees in front of Rusty, then spoke to Rusty. "Well, boy, we got it to do. It ain't gonna be easy on either of us, but I think we hafta get it done." He reined his friend into the trees and moved toward the nearest draw and the cut he would make through the timber. With a glance to the sun, he guessed he would reach the camp of the raiders just about dusk.

# CHAPTER 22

## STEALTH

He dropped off his promontory to the dry creek below him, followed the creek through a cut at a low-rising ridge, and kept to the creek bottom until a notch showed in the ridge above him to the west. He cut through the trees to push to the crest of the higher ridge. It was a difficult route for most forests with tall pines and spruce that would stretch as tall as a hundred feet, some of the spruce stretching to over two hundred feet or more, there was also considerable dead-fall, but the dim trail taken by wild game offered a twist-ing, winding way to the top. Once atop the ridge, he took the time for another scan with his binoculars, and after picking his route off the ridge into the valley below, he nudged the big stallion to take the dim trail, pulling taut on the lead rope of the grey. A flash of black in the timber told of Lobo's following and Eli grinned at the tenacity of the pup.

The trail dropped into the bottom of Bear Creek and Eli followed it down to the saddle crossing he had chosen from his promontory. He picketed the horses in the trees near the creek and grass, but well under cover. He checked his pistols, felt for his Bowie in the sheath at his back, and slipped the Winchester Yellowboy from the scabbard, checked the load and reached into the saddlebags for a handful of additional ammo. A glance at the lowering sun and he started to the trees to make his way to the crest of this hill and saddle crossing, knowing the suspected camp of the raiders lay in the basin beyond.

He guessed he had come over four miles since his first sighting from the promontory and the steady climb up the timbered ridge had him winded. He dropped to his haunches under the widespread branches of a big spruce and stretched out his legs for one last look before the fading light was lost. By line of sight, he was less than a mile from the camp that lay in the basin below this ridge and behind the bigger hill where Eli had spotted their lookout. The horses were corralled behind the camp in a narrow draw, lean-tos had been fashioned by the men, and they had a single cookfire that showed in the dim light.

He started down the steep, timbered slope, keeping behind the bigger trees and watching every step. The hillside was mostly trees and any open area had bunchgrass or aspen, but the rocky soil made Eli extra cautious, for all he needed was to send a stone tumbling to start a rockslide that would give away his presence. He smelled the smoke from their cookfire and paused beside a big ponderosa, keeping himself near the rusty-colored bark of the big tree, trying to fade into the natural cover, just in case there was anyone making a trip into the woods to answer the call of nature.

Dusk had dropped its curtain of darkness and shadows filled the emptiness between the hills and among the trees. Eli was about thirty yards from the edge of their camp, and he dropped to his stomach beside the ponderosa, fading into the deep pine needles and watching. As the men busied themselves with fixing their meal, some cleaning weapons, others sitting idly or dozing while they waited to be called for their supper. There were no horses nearby, apparently all had been taken to the corral. Eli thought of the habit of the Natives, always keeping their favorite pony near their lodge, ready to hand if needed. But these men showed no concern, probably never imagining anyone, Native or other, that would dare attack them.

He crawled closer to a group of three men that were talking as they cleaned weapons or sharpened knives. Belly down behind a small cluster of rocks between some trees, Eli listened to the men brag about their debauchery during their attack on the wagons. One boasted of his taking a woman and cutting her throat to bleed out while he used her. The others laughed and did what evil men always do and tried to best their companion with their own tales of evildoings. The nagging thought that Eli had harbored about being certain these were the guilty men, was dispelled as he listened to their tales of wickedness.

This was not the first time Eli had marveled at how men could yield themselves to such evil as these men had done. He had seen death and destruction in the war, but this depth of debauchery and evil outweighed the worst of the war. Anger and bile rose in Eli as he lay in the darkness, looking around the camp at the other men, counting ten men, plus at least one on the mountain on lookout and with one or two having the look of Natives but the dress of white men. He backed away and moved to the far side of the camp, wanting to hear the conversation of two men that had separated themselves from the others and had the manner of leaders.

It took Eli a good quarter hour, maybe a little more, to get to the far side of the camp, choosing stealth to haste. As he moved through the thicket of aspen, he was as silent as the wind, picking his path on the matted and wet leaves of the quakies, but moved away from the white-barked aspen as he neared the men, choosing to use the low branches and dark trunks of the spruce and fir for cover. He bellied down and slowly crawled closer and heard their voices but had to be closer to understand. A clump of scrub oak offered him cover and he moved close.

"That bunch o' freighters should be showin' up any day, mebbe e'en tomorrow," growled the bigger of the two men. He had the cavalry britches of the Confederates, tall boots, and the campaign hat of an officer. Eli frowned, thinking that most men had put the war behind them and were doing their best to rid themselves of any vestiges of remembrance, but there were always those that reveled in their deeds or misdeeds, and with someone like this whose morals and character were nonexistent, he probably had not even been in the war but liked to make others think he was a veteran of the war. He had met others that were pretenders rather than contenders and none of them had enough backbone to last through any real battle.

The second man answered, "Hittin' that wagon train wasn't the smartest thing we've done. If any of those had survived and lived to tell anyone, our lives wouldn't be worth spit!"

"Oh quit'cher whinin'. Lettin' a little blood an' havin' some fun keeps the boys happy. They was gettin' restless just waitin' on them freighters! An' I ain't tellin' 'em what we're after till we gets it, neither. If'n some o' them knew, they'd already be plottin' how they could get it all fer themselves!"

"Whatsamatta, don'tchu like them thinkin' like you?" cackled the second man. He was a lean, lantern jawed, slovenly sort, with long, stringy hair, bushy beard, piercing eyes, and always appeared to be drooling tobacco juice through his beard. He had a short-bladed sword through his belt that looked like the point had been broken off, but the blade had many scars from both the sharpening stone and its use for some kind of wickedness. Both men had pistols, the first man, Silas Farley, had an army issue belt and holster that held his Remington Army, and the second man, Wallace 'Wally' Ainsley, had his Remington stuffed in his belt on the opposite side of his sword that would allow him to cross draw both weapons.

Silas growled at Wally, shaking his head, "Watch'ur tongue 'fore I cut it off!"

Wally dropped his hands to his weapons, glared at Silas, and said, "Just try it an' I'll cut ever'thing off'n you, like I did that pilgrim!" he cackled.

Silas stood and looked beyond the campfire, "They switchin' lookouts?"

"Tha's what you tol'em to do!" answered Wally. "Dunno what they're gonna see after dark anyhow!" he grumbled.

"Heck an' Amos said they'd build up the fires right big when they got near, so the lookout should spot the fires o' the freighters. An' if'n he does, he's s'posed to come tell us. That way we can hit 'em 'fore they get aroun' in the mornin'."

"An' if'n he don't?"

"Then we'll hafta wait till we see 'em. That'll give us

time to get in place to ambush 'em like we planned,"
answered Silas, shaking his head, believing he was
captaining a bunch of dummies.

When Eli heard the names of the two teamsters that
traveled with Sid, he grit his teeth in anger, knowing
those two were as guilty of the massacre as the others.
He watched as the men began moseying toward the
cookfire, anxious to eat and have their coffee. When they
moved away, Eli slowly crabbed back from the brush into
the trees and walked back into the deeper woods to
conjure up some kind of plan. As he considered the
camp, the number of raiders and their positions around
the camp, he began to make his plan, but nagging in the
back of his mind was the lookout, if he heard any shooting, he would come running and there was no way of
knowing if there was one or two and where or when they
would come into the fight.

He considered his adversary, knowing the old adage
about crooks or outlaws being men that are too lazy to
work an honest job or occupation, and being outlaws,
they try to do things the easy way or leave them undone.
He thought about the layout of the camp, where each of
the lean-tos were and how many men were in each
shelter and those that slept under the trees. What he was
planning would be considered by some to be murder, but
he saw it as little different than an act of war against a
cruel and vicious enemy, an enemy that had shown his
evil nature to be one that needed to be destroyed.

Eli recalled many times before he was in command,
that his duty required him to make a stealthy approach
and eliminate the enemy without alerting the band of
marauders. He remembered the times he and the
Cheyenne scout, Plenty Coups, had to infiltrate the
village of the Sioux or the Crow and either take a captive

or take the life of an enemy. He knew he would need all those acquired skills this night, for he was one against many, and every one of these were vicious and evil men without any shame or limit to their debauchery.

He crawled under the wide, low limbs of a big spruce and stretched out on his back, his clasped hands behind his head, and began mentally mapping the camp, the men, and what and how he would make his attack. As he closed his eyes, trying to relax, he sensed rather than knew a presence. Without breathing or moving, he opened his eyes and saw a shadow come from behind the big trunk of the spruce and recognized the scent before he saw Lobo, belly crawling close to his side. The wolf reached up, lay his chin on Eli's stomach, and rolled his eyes to look at his friend. Eli chuckled to himself, lowered his hand to stroke Lobo's head and rub behind his ears, realizing the presence of his friend had allowed him to relax, if even for a few moments.

He waited until a little before midnight, then rolled from under the tree and in a low crouch, worked his way to his first target. Two men had stretched out their blankets on the far side of a cluster of scrub oak and were separated from the rest of the camp. The men were about six feet apart, one on his back and snorting and snoring, but facing the brush. The other was in the clear, laying on his side with his back to his companion, his blanket on the thick carpet of ponderosa needles. Eli looked to the men, their heads toward the trees, and crawled closer to them, moving behind the side-sleeper. He rose behind the man, scooted closer and in one swift move clasped a hand over the man's mouth and drove the Bowie knife to its hilt into his heart. He twisted the blade side to side, holding the man tight to the ground with his weight on his shoulders until he moved no more. Eli wiped his blade on the man's trousers as he turned to the second man, recognizing him as the one that bragged about slitting the throat of one of the women. Eli was on hands and feet as he moved toward the man, then lunged to straddle the noisy sleeper, cover his mouth, and slit his throat ear to ear. The man's eyes flared showing fear and trying to shout a warning, but he choked on his own blood, and Eli whispered, "How does it feel to have your throat cut like you did that woman?" The man tried to squirm, but Eli drove the blade of the Bowie into his middle, just below the left rib and knew he had found the man's heart. He glared hatred at the man, twisting the knife back and forth to destroy his heart and take his life. The monster stilled, eyes frozen wide open with fear, as his haunted spirit whispered through the trees.

Eli looked over the brush to the rest of the camp, no one stirred, the sounds of noisy sleepers filling the void of darkness. The fading fire glowed just enough to show one man sit up, looking around with fear-filled wide eyes as he batted at the darkness, mumbled something and fell back, to roll to his side and resume his rattling snore.

# CHAPTER 23

## HELLFIRE

Eli crawled through the grass and pine needles, using the grasses to wipe the blood from his hands and clothes as he returned to the trees where he left his rifle. Lobo was belly down beside the rifle and lifted his head as Eli returned. Eli dropped to his knee to rub the scruff of the wolf's neck, and whisper to the pup, "Good boy, Lobo, good boy. You stay now, stay." With rifle in hand, he started for the other end of the camp where the lean-tos were tucked into the edge of the trees and watched the dimly lit camp through the trees. He moved back toward the raiders' horse corral and quietly lowered the poles and cut the ropes, opening the end of the corral nearest the camp, knowing the horses would head down the draw toward the camp if they were spooked for any reason. The moon was in its first quarter and the stars gave the sliver little help to light the land, but Eli was accustomed to the night and could make out the lean-tos and the long legs of several of the men that extended beyond the edge of the cover.

One man crawled from his shelter, looked back into

the dark pine boughs, and shook his head. Eli could hear the whistling snores of the man left behind and understood the disgust of his shelter partner, who walked to the cookfire, checked the coffeepot, and walked to the river to get more water. Eli took advantage of the solitary figure and quickly slit another throat and silenced the snoring of the big man, who kicked his feet but once before he choked on his own blood and died.

The solitary figure at the fire tended his coffeepot and glanced back to his lean-to, shook his head as he realized his partner was no longer snoring, but turned his attention back to the coffeepot. Eli stood his Winchester behind a tree, looked at the man at the fire, and started walking to the cookfire, rubbing his eyes and grumbling as if he just awoke and mumbled, "Got'ny coffee goin'?"

The man at the fire did not turn, but grunted, "Yeah, but git'chur own cup!" Those were his last words as he crumpled beside the fire, blood spilling from his throat and chest as he kicked his last. Eli poured himself a cup of coffee, stood with his back to the fire and looked about the camp. No one stirred and he casually strolled back toward the lean-tos and into the trees.

There were six more men in the camp and one, maybe two lookouts. The others were two to a shelter and were too close to kill one without waking the other. Eli slipped the Winchester over his shoulder, the sling holding it tight to his back, and walked back to the cookfire. He grabbed the shovel that was used to move the coals and snuff out the fire, and scooped up a shovel full of fiery coals and started to the edge of the camp where the dry grass was tall and stood between the trail and the creek and scattered the coals about. He returned for another shovel full and added to the first beginnings of a grass fire. He tossed the shovel in the creek, padded away into the darkness, and went to the trees, taking up his preselected position. He knew it was a risk to start a fire in the thick timber, but he hoped the creek and the trail would contain the flames and prevent any spread. But he also knew the death and destruction already caused and could be caused by this band of cutthroats would rival the damage of any forest fire, and if these men could know the horrors of hellfire, so much the better.

Eli had hustled about and gathered dead branches, limbs, and anything that could add to the fire and piled it up to fuel the flames toward the shelters. He started walking around the camp, working toward the upper end, all the while watching the fire grow and raise its hoary head of flames to snap at the covers of the sleeping men. He heard one of the men scream, saw him scramble from his cover and start shouting, "FIRE, FIRE, FIRE! Wake up! Ever'thin's on fire!" he screamed.

Eli started to the horse corral at a run, Lobo beside him, and started to spook the horses, but the scent of the wolf carried by the breeze that was fanning the flames was enough and the horses spooked, many rearing and screaming, pawing at the night sky. They started crowding toward the opening, realized it was open, then charged through. Eli shouted, screamed, and waved his arms to add to the confusion and pandemonium. He watched as the horses stampeded toward the camp, fought one another to get away from the flames, and crashed through the woods to follow the creek out of the hills. The smoke of the fire and the dust of the stampede hung like a cloud over the camp yet revealed at least one body that had been trampled by the horses, but the flames were devouring everything in sight. Men ran, screaming, cursing, shouting, a few trying to beat at the flames with their blankets, making a sight of themselves fighting the fire in their ragged, faded red union suits with rear flaps hanging open.

Eli leaned against a big tree, watching the melee and laughing at the antics of the frightened and angry men as they fought vainly trying to put out the fire, knowing all their gear, including their clothes and weapons, was in danger of being burnt to ashes. He shook his head, watching, saw the flames dwindling and smoke and dust enveloping the camp, and reached down to stroke the head of the wolf pup, and said, "Maybe we better leave now, you think?"

He circled wide of the camp but heard one of the men cry out, "Hey! Homer an' Charlie got their throats cut! Who'd a dun' that?"

Eli changed his mind and jacked a round into the chamber of the Winchester and screamed like a banshee letting his god-awful wail carry over the crackling of the fire and picked his first target, dropped the hammer, and saw a stinking raider fall face first into the flames adding to the stench of the fire. The single shot was not alarming for the flames were licking at the lean-tos where the men's weapons were cached, and bullets started exploding in the blaze. Cackling and shouting with a hideous scream, Eli added to the pandemonium as the raiders thought hell itself had come calling. One of the men grabbed his rifle and started shooting into the darkness, yelling taunts, "C'mon devil, I ain't afeerd o' you!"

Eli recognized him as the one called Silas and thought to be the leader. Stepping behind a big ponderosa, Eli turned back toward the firelit camp, lifted his rifle and waited for the screamer to show himself. He stood in the open, firing into the darkness of the woods, shouting his taunts and Eli took a steady aim, squeezed off his shot, and saw the man stagger back. Eli sent another bullet and blood blossomed on Silas's chest. The raider dropped his rifle, looked down at the blood, lifted his haunted face to the darkness and wide-eyed, dropped to his knees and fell forward on his face, unmoving.

Eli and Lobo took off at a trot into the thicker timber that hugged the slope of the hill he had crossed earlier. He laughed as he started up the side slope, keeping in the trees, glancing over his shoulder at the fading flames and the rising smoke of the devastated camp of the renegades. He paused and turned to look back, he knew there were two or three others, but they were the followers and with no one to lead, and death and hell to follow, he thought they would waste little time catching up some horses and skedaddling.

————

ELI SAT ATOP RUSTY, leaning on his pommel, as he watched the first of the freight wagons round the bend before him. Sid was well ahead of the wagons and spotted Eli and his horses to the side of the road in the shade of the towering spruce trees. Sid gigged his mount forward, anxious to get the report from Eli. He lifted a hand high in greeting and reined up beside the big stallion. Sid stretched out his hand, "Good to see you, my friend! And all in one piece I see."

Eli grinned as he shook hands with Sid, "And it's not for lack of them tryin', I'll have you know."

Sid frowned, "You found 'em?"

"You might say that," answered Eli as he nudged Rusty from the shade and motioned to Sid with a nod of his head and the two men took to the road ahead of the wagons. Eli nodded up the road, "Just around the bend there you'll see some of their handiwork. When I found that, I tracked 'em a ways, learned somethin' and taught somethin'." He shook his head at the remembrance of the last two days, "Don't think you'll have too much trouble, but there's somethin' you need to settle."

"What's that?" asked Sid, scowling as he looked at Eli.

"You've got a couple your men that are in league with the Confederate outlaws."

Sid reined up, turned, and looked at Eli, "How do you know and who are they?" he growled with resentment and anger at the thought that men he trusted and worked with could betray his trust and be involved in something that could destroy him, even kill him. He glanced back to the wagons at least a half-mile behind, and leaned toward Eli, waiting for his answer.

# CHAPTER 24

## REVELATION

The freighters slowed as the burnt wagons came into view, the scattered remains that included pieces of clothing and other personal items, told of the massacre. As they passed the remnants, no one shouted, cursed, or even cracked a whip. The mules were pushed on with nothing more than a slap of the lines on their rumps while the teamsters and roustabouts looked silently at the mute evidence that lay before them. This was not the first time they had seen the results of a deadly attack, but this was recent, not something from the war, and most assumed this was the result of Indians, but there were no scalped and mutilated bodies, just the cross that Eli had fashioned from burnt timbers from the wagons and stuck in the ground at the crest of the little knoll where the mass grave lay. The smell of smoke, death, and burnt flesh lay low on the grasses and in the trees, stirred by the passing of the freighter, and each man recognized the smells, and Eli noticed as they lifted neckerchiefs to cover their mouth and nose, revulsed by the smells of death.

Eli and Sid had drawn to the side to watch the men as they passed. They sat silent, unmoving, but watching. The only movement was the swish of their horses' tails as they attempted to chase away the flying pests that had gathered at the massacre. As the horses rocked from side to side, shifting their weight from one hoof to the other, Eli and Sid leaned forward on their pommels, faces somber, and anger flaring in their eyes.

The rattle of trace chains, the clatter of hooves, the creak of wheels, and the groan of the wagons sung a hymn of sorrow that almost seemed sacrilegious, but all the while a mute testimony of those that had struggled to come this far, only to meet this horrible end. The four freighters passed and were followed by the remuda of mules and horses, driven by two of the roustabouts. Eli looked at Sid, and they nudged their mounts to the trail. They would be stopping soon for their midday meal and rest for the mules at one of the many crossings of the Naches, and Sid trusted his lead driver to pick a good site where they could pull off the road and give the animals some graze.

The sun was high overhead and Eli shaded his eyes as he looked at it and back to the wagons that had drawn to the side. The men were already gathering some wood for a small cookfire for their coffee and to heat up the leftovers from their breakfast. Eli had explained to Sid what he had heard from the raiders and now Sid had to force himself to act no differently around the men, especially the two named by Eli. Because of the depleted numbers of the raiders, they did not expect any attack by the remnants, but the traitors would not know that, and Eli expected them to unknowingly give themselves away when they camped for the night.

Sᴍᴅ ᴀɴᴅ Eʟɪ led the way, leading the wagons by about a half-mile, and Eli nodded, "That blaze on the tree yonder will probably mark the spot for the camp. If you look yonder," nodding upstream and to the taller hills on the north side, "that bald-topped hill is where the look-outs were and from there, they can see right into this campsite. If you're lettin' Heck pick the spot, you can bet this is what he'll choose."

"But, when they get here it'll be a little early to stop. We try to make all the miles we can 'fore stoppin'. He knows that," replied Sid, frowning but with a glimmer of hope that Eli was wrong about his lead teamster.

"He'll have trouble with his wagon, maybe a squeaky wheel that needs grease or..." He shrugged. "But I'm goin' up on that hill where I can see into their camp. If there's anyone left, maybe they'll be around, or some sign of them. I don't think there will be, but maybe they got some more raiders that were hid out somewhere."

"I'll come with you. I wanna see that camp, too," growled Sid, with a glance over his shoulder to see if the wagons were coming, but they were out of sight around a bend in the road. He looked at Eli and nudged his mount away from the road to follow his scout.

At the crest of the rise, they left the horses in the trees and walked to a rocky escarpment. Eli dropped to his haunches and slipped the binoculars from the case. The black scar in the basin marked the campsite and Eli focused in on the scene. The bodies lay where they fell and although there was sign of either man or horses that had meandered through the scene, there was no move-ment, no sign of campfires or gathering of goods. Turkey buzzards were still picking at the remains, two coyotes had commandeered one for themselves and furtively watched the buzzards as they tried to tear tidbits from the carcass. "They're all gone," stated Eli as he lowered the binoculars and passed them to Sid.

As Sid scanned the burnt battleground, he groaned, mumbled, and said, "Remind me to never get on your bad side," and chuckled. "You made a mess of that bunch, that's fer sure an' certain." He lowered the binoculars, looked at Eli, "How many were there?"

"Ten, plus one or two lookouts."

"And you kilt how many?" asked an incredulous Sid.

"Maybe eight or so, I think. All I could think of was the bodies of the women and children that had been used and slaughtered. When the fire raged, I let 'em think the devil had brought his hellfire for 'em." He chuckled as he remembered, "You shoulda seen 'em runnin' aroun' in their long johns, flaps open, and them tryin' to put out that fire with their blankets. But even that wasn't enough for that bunch of baby killin' varmints. If I coulda killed each of 'em twiced, it still wouldn't be enough," growled Eli, smacking his fist in his palm and gritting his teeth. He looked at Sid, "If you coulda seen 'em, you'd be thinkin' the same thing, too."

Sid lowered the glasses again, turned to look at Eli, "I ain't never been one for killin' an' such. That's why I never went into the war, but that don't mean I hate what they done any less."

"And those two with the wagons are just as guilty as every man that slit a woman's or child's throat!" snarled Eli, his anger rising even more.

"Ummhmm," answered Sid, rising to return to the horses. Eli followed and both mounted, started back down the hill, and stopped as they came to the road. A quick glance back toward the debated campsite showed the wagons pulling off the road and toward the trees. Sid glanced back to Eli, looked up at the lowering sun, "We still got at least an hour, mebbe two, of daylight. And he's stoppin' just like you said."

"Ummhmm," answered Eli, reining Rusty to the road.

———

IT WAS customary to have two cookfires and the men chosen as cooks were busy at their work. Nothing unusual was happening and Sid and Eli sat apart from the others where Eli made his separate camp. Sid looked at Eli, "I don't see 'em doin' anything different yet," drawled Sid, looking toward the cookfires of the men.

"It's early yet, not even full dark. From what I heard, it'll be 'fore they turn in for the night," explained Eli, pushing his coffeepot closer to the flames of his small fire. He looked to the others, saw most of the men gathered near the cookfires, but two men walked about, working their way along the bank of the river, appearing to talk and amble along as if there was nothing amiss. Eli thought he recognized the two men, but turned to Sid, and asked, "Those two down by the river, is that Heck Philpot and Amos Acker?"

Sid looked, stood, and walked around the fire as if gathering more wood and looked below to see the two men by the willows and looked back at Eli, "Yeah, that's them."

"Weren't they two of the men that you said were Southerners?" asked Eli.

"Yeah, but that don't make 'em guilty of anything," defended Sid, still not wanting to believe any of his men were sellouts.

Eli cut the last of his back strap meat into steaks and

hung them over the fire to broil. With the last of his potatoes in the coals, and the coffee perking, he sat back to await the feast that he would share with Sid. "So, Sid, when those two show themselves and we know without a doubt they were part of the plan to take over these wagons, what're you gonna do with 'em?"

"I dunno. Course, they weren't part of the bunch that massacred that wagon train, at least not when it happened, but if you hadn't done in the pack o' coyotes, they woulda done the same thing to all of us. So, are they guilty of the same thing?" he asked, looking to Eli for his answer.

"Well, we can't hang somebody for what they might have done, or what they were gonna do…" He shrugged as he checked the broiling steaks. "But ain't that what they call 'guilt by association'? You know, they woulda been a part of it all if they hadn't been with us."

Sid frowned, "So, does God condemn us for what we think, or what we do?"

Eli showed his consternation, looked up at Sid, "There ya' go, preachin' the Word!"

"Well, ain't that the way it is? I mean, God says our thoughts ain't always the best, but I don't think he condemns us just for thinkin' somethin', does He?" asked Sid.

"I think it's in Proverbs, long about number 23 or so where He says, *For as he thinketh in his heart, so is he.*"

"Yeah, well, let's just wait and see what they do when we confront 'em with everything," resolved Sid, accepting the offered willow with the steak dripping its juices.

The men had walked away from the fire with their plates and cups full and gathered in groups of two and three to enjoy their meal. Again, Eli noticed the two men, Heck and Amos, were together and apart from the others, seated on the tongue of a wagon with their backs to the woods and beside one another and watching the rest of the teamsters and roustabouts. The dim light of dusk had faded, and the stars were lighting their lanterns, the sliver of the first quarter of moon hanging like a scoop in the eastern sky.

Eli looked at the two and watched as they ambled toward the stream to rinse out their plates and cups and walk back to the fading cookfires. With a glance around at the others, they put away their stuff and separated, Heck staying by that fire and Amos going to the other. When Amos looked back to Heck, the big man nodded and both began stacking more wood on the fires, stepping back as they flared up and holding their hands to the flames as if they were just warming themselves. When no one protested, they added more wood. One of the teamsters hollered, "Hey, what're you doin'? That wood's fer in the mornin'!"

Heck answered with a growl, "I'm cold! I'll get more wood later!" He glanced to Amos, nodded, and both men added even more wood. The fires flared high, casting light about the camp, and Eli glanced to Sid, saw him shaking his head as he watched the two men show themselves to be the sellouts he feared. With a nod to Eli, Sid rose and started toward the first fire, Eli followed close behind, watching the other teamsters as they rolled out their blankets, making their beds and more, anticipating a good night's sleep. But several had looked back to Heck, frowning, knowing it was not a cold night and there was no reason for a big fire. Eli saw several of the men turn to face the fires and stand with hands on hips, waiting for something to happen.

# Chapter 25

## Decision

S id walked to the fire where Heck was warming himself and called out to the others, "Hey you men, ever'body, gather round here, we got some-thin' to talk about!" He stood, hands high, motioning to the others to come near. As they gathered, Eli held back away from the fire on the rim of darkness, watching Heck and Amos. As the men settled about, most sitting on the rocks or logs nearby, others standing near, all looked to Sid.

Sid looked around at everyone, and began, "Y'all remember those wagons we passed earlier, the ones that had been burnt out and such?" Most of the men nodded, some grunting or mumbling their having seen the remains.

"That was a wagon train of settlers, five or six fami-lies, with women and children. They were set upon by outlaw raiders, an' the men were kilt, some burned alive, and the women were used badly before they had their throats slit, an' the children also." He paused, looking around, until one of the men that was seated, asked, "How come you know all that, Sid?"

"Because Eli, our scout, came upon the wagons shortly after it happened. He's the one that buried them on the hill near there. You saw where the burnt cross was? That's where they were buried."

"Wal, who done it?" asked another, "An' are they still around hereabouts?"

"It was a band of Confederate raiders, a bunch o' wannabe guerrillas that were after our wagons. We think they thought that train was ours and they hit it, but what they did, well, there ain't no excusin' that!"

The men looked at one another, mumbling their agreement with Sid and sharing their thoughts about what had been done, especially to the women and children. Sid raised his hands for quiet and started to continue, but one of the men asked, "How you know it was Confederates, coulda been just 'bout anybody!" he looked at the other men for their agreement, but there was little or no response. He turned back to face Sid for an answer.

"Coulda been, but it weren't. The leader was a man name o' Silas Farley," Sid paused and looked at Heck and Amos, saw them getting a little fidgety, but continued, "an' his right-hand man was named Wallace Ainsley." He paused again, seeing frowns and questions on the faces of the men, then continued. "Now, here's the problem. Those men were after our wagons, 'cuz what you don't know, is we have more'n flour and such in these wagons. There's a considerable amount of gold, placer gold, from the diggin's up Bear Gulch back in Montana Territory. We're transportin' it to Fort Steilacoom."

"But, if they're after the gold, won't they be comin' after us, and purty soon?" asked the same inquisitive

man that was seated on the big rock, looking about at
the others as he spoke.

Sid continued, "Well, you see. That's what these big
fires are all about. Heck and Amos aren't cold, they're a
part of the bunch of outlaw raiders! And these fires are a
signal to the outlaws!" He was looking directly at Heck
when he revealed what was happening and saw Heck's
expression of anger and fear.

Heck stepped back, arms outstretched to his sides,
and said, "That's a lie! We ain't part o' them! We was
just cold! Me'n Amos there was down by the river and
it's cold there. We's just tryin' to get warm." He looked
about at the others, fear showing on his face. Eli saw him
grabbing at a holstered pistol at his side and the men
began to scatter. The Colt appeared in Eli's hand as he
stepped forward, slightly behind Heck, but he also
watched Amos, who had turned away and started toward
the wagons.

Heck hollered, "Get back! I'm tellin' ya, we ain't part
o' that!" he waved his pistol about, and the men took to
the wagons, the darkness cloaking them as they ran.
Heck looked at Sid who stood, hands out to his sides and
looking directly at Heck. "You, tell 'em it ain't so! Ain't
no way you could know that! Ain't nobody said nuthin'!"
he declared, little realizing he was admitting to his
deception. He turned to face Sid, growling, "I oughta just
shoot you now an' be done wit' it!" cocking the hammer
of his Remington Army pistol as he spoke.

But the same sound came from behind him as Eli
said, "Don't do it, Heck. I'll do you just like I did Silas
and the others!"

But Heck had never been one to back down, he had
been the bully that could beat every man, whether it was
rough-and-tumble, with knives, or with pistols. He had

never been beaten and he began to growl, "Ain't no man ever beat me. I'm gonna kill you an' gut you," he was glowering at Sid, "and then I'll do the same thing to your scout, who thinks he's so high an' mighty."

Heck lifted the muzzle of the Remington, but before he could pull the trigger, the eyes of Sid told Eli to shoot, and Eli dropped the hammer on Heck. But Eli had intentionally aimed the Colt at Heck's upper leg, hoping to knock him off his aim and not kill him. The bullet tore through Heck's butt and into his hip joint, knocking him to the side and his pistol fired into the air as Heck screamed, falling to his side. He twisted to the side, bringing the pistol to bear on Eli, but before he could trigger the Remington, Eli's second shot bore into Heck's chest, blossoming red in the firelight and tearing through his torso to rip its way out, breaking his clavicle and boring into the dirt. Wide eyes looked at Eli, but there was no life in them. He fell to his side, dead where he lay.

Eli quickly turned to look for Amos, but he had disappeared into the night. He turned to see Sid, kneeling beside the body of Heck, and shaking his head. He looked up at Eli, "Thanks. He was set to kill me, after most of three years together and me trustin' him as the lead teamster. I didn't wanna believe it." He stood, looking around, looked to Eli, "Amos?"

Eli pursed his lips, shook his head, "Dunno. He took off when the shootin' was about to start. Didn't see where he went."

One of the teamsters, Virgil Appleton, one of the men Sid had said was a Southerner, came close, pointed to the wagons near the trees, "I saw him over by that last wagon. He was just sittin' on the tongue, lookin' into the trees, mumblin' to himself." He paused, looked at the body of Heck, and added, "I ain't none surprised 'bout him," pointing to Heck with his chin, "but I'm thinkin' if Amos had anything to do with it, Heck made him."

Sid and Eli looked at him, and with a glance to Heck, Sid agreed, "You know, that sounds 'bout right. Amos weren't no more'n nine stone compared to Heck's sixteen stone or more. Wouldn't take much from a bully like Heck to make Amos do just about anything, an' most li'lns look up to the big'ns like they was heroes or sumpin."

"Well, you do whatever you think is right, you're the boss. But I ain't turnin' my back on nobody for a long time. Not after what I saw and had to deal with," answered Eli, starting to his camp to get away from the others. He went to his blankets and was surprised to see Lobo stretched out on them. He lay on his back, paws in the air, and paid no attention to Eli as he dropped down beside him. Eli rubbed the pup's belly, pushed him aside, and stretched out on the nice warm blankets, compliments of Lobo.

————

ELI SAT atop the rocky outcrop that overlooked the camp when the coming of day split the black of night from the grey of early morn. The slow coming of the sun continued to push back the curtain of darkness as the stars snuffed out their lanterns, and Eli talked with his Lord as he watched the first light of day. He made his quick survey of the outlying countryside, saw nothing amiss, and dropped off the rocks to make his sliding descent of the escarpment. When he stepped from the trees to his camp, he grinned to see Sid pouring himself a cup of coffee from Eli's pot.

"Is there any left for me?" asked Eli, leaning his rifle against the log and reaching for his cup.

"Of course, there's at least a swallow or two," answered a grinning Sid.

Eli poured his coffee, sat down opposite Sid, and asked, "So, now what?"

Sid chuckled, "We keep goin', that's what. I let my number two man, Reginald Culpepper, Reg for short, take over Heck's place as lead teamster, and I'm lettin' Amos stay. I think he'll be alright, now that he's seen the error of his ways." He took a drink of coffee, lowered the cup, and looked at Eli, "I want you to continue your scout, 'cuz there could be others of this same bunch that we don't know about, or others just as mean, and I ain't willin' to part with any of our cargo."

"You think tellin' the men was smart?" asked Eli, referring to the cargo of gold.

"Yeah, an' when I tol' 'em this mornin' there'd be a bonus for all of 'em, they was happy 'bout that. So, I think we'll do alright."

"Like I said before, you're the boss," answered Eli, sipping his coffee as he looked over the rim at his friend.

# CHAPTER 26

## SUMMIT

The shoulders of the mountains pushed in against the narrow canyon of the Naches River causing every sound to be magnified and often echoing across the narrows. The shouts of the teamsters, the crack of the whips, the bray of the mules, and the creak of the wagons sounded long and strong as the big mules strained against the traces. The climb was hard, often steep, forcing the mules to lean into their task and the teamsters to call on their teams, encouraging, cursing, slapping their rumps with the lines, and cracking the whips over their heads, all in an effort to surmount the next rise.

Eli and Sid had been in the lead but often stopped to look back, ensuring the wagons were still coming, nothing was wrong, and to give their own mounts a brief rest. Sid looked to Eli, "Ain't much further now, should hit the park 'fore noon. It's the downgrade that's got me a little worried, those wagons are heavy, and that road is mighty steep!"

"You been over this pass before, how many times?" asked Eli.

"Only onct, but it weren't with wagons as heavy as these," replied Sid, worry showing on his face. "They say it were the Hudson Bay Comp'ny that came o'er this pass the first time, leastwise the first white men, but that was nigh unto thirty plus years back. It's been used since 'fore the war by wagon trains, cattle herds, an' more. But nowadays, many are goin' the way of Snoqualmie. It's further, but easier." He paused as they moved back to the road to lead the way for the wagons. "You'll see what I mean when we take a look in a bit."

The sun was high overhead when the wagons pulled into the park-like setting called Summit Prairie. It was a wide, flat park with tall grasses and easy breezes. Sid said, "We'll stay here till mornin', give the mules a break, the men too. It'll take a long day tomorrow to get down off'n here."

Eli reined up, motioned to Sid toward the trees, "There's somethin' movin' over there," said Eli, his voice low as he leaned forward, twisting side to side to try to see through the thick trees. Big spruce and fir were standing tall, trunks bigger than a man could span, stretching into the heavens for a hundred feet, give or take, and the shadows were thick with random lances of sunlight giving the only light. As he watched, he recognized the movement, "Those are horses, loose horses! What are..." and he answered his own question, "I'm thinkin' those are some of the bunch from the raiders. I ran 'em off during the fight. They prob'ly followed the few men left behind when they caught up some and took off."

"Could be," replied Sid. "How 'bout you checkin' it out 'fore I let the men get down."

Eli nodded and nudged the stallion forward, tossing the lead line of the grey packhorse to Sid. He pushed into the trees, looking about and checking the tracks. He moved further, following the horses, and saw them stopped in a little clearing, heads down, grazing on the tall grass. He sat in the shade, watching the animals, saw no sign of alarm, no other sign of men, and returned to the park and the wagons. Eli waved to Sid for an all-clear sign and picked out a place for his own camp away from the others.

He chose a spot where there was a break in the trees and a small clearing beyond. He stepped down and began to strip the gear from the horses, looking about as he moved. He frowned when he saw fresh dirt and paused his actions to check out the spot. He pushed the dirt around with his foot and uncovered what had been a campfire, and he could tell it was fresh, probably the night before and the camp was vacated just this morning. He stood, looking around and saw a stack of wood, and beyond that another patch of fresh-turned soil, only this spot was larger and near the trees. His first thought was this was a grave, but one hastily dug and covered. Most would cover the fresh-turned soil with rocks to keep any predators or carrion eaters away, but there were no stones, no marker.

He grabbed the shovel from the packs and went to the mound. It took only a few moments to uncover enough to see this was a grave and the body was that of a man. He brushed away some of the dirt to recognize this was one of the raiders, probably wounded by Eli's bullet and died here when they fled the scene. Eli shook his head, covered the body, and walked back to the horses to finish stripping off the gear.

When he finished, he gathered some firewood,

prepared to make a fire, but his curiosity got the best of him, and he began searching the park for sign of the raiders. As he walked about, he saw several tracks of horses and men, as near as he could make out there were at least four men, maybe five, and the same number of horses. He thought the loose horses had probably followed this bunch from below, for horses are a social animal, used to being in the company of familiar companions, but the wild horses showed no sign of wanting to leave this park area where there was water, graze, and shelter. Yet the tracks of the ridden horses had left this area probably this morning, and they were headed west.

Eli walked to the camp of the teamsters looking for Sid and once spotted, he motioned to the man to join him at his camp away from the others. When Sid came through the trees, Eli motioned him to the log as he prepared the pot of water to make some coffee. Once the fire was going, Eli nodded to the grave at the edge of the trees, "That's one of the raiders. They buried him this morning before they left, and there's more of 'em than I thought."

Sid frowned, "How many more?"

"Looks to be four or five, enough that if they want to make another try and if they got the guts to do it, they could," answered Eli. "I'm gonna go up on that knob yonder, have a good look around, see if I can see anything. Might even make a reconnoiter tonight."

Sid sighed heavily, staring into the small flames of the fire, and looked at Eli, "That's all we need, another attack. Guess I need to tell the men," he drawled, watching the coffeepot begin its dance on the rock.

"Might wanna make sure they're well-armed too," suggested Eli. "This is rough country, lots of hideouts, and I could miss 'em. If I do, they could hit the wagons by complete surprise and cause a ruckus that'd be hard to fight."

"Yeah, that's what I'm afeerd of!" growled Sid, accepting a cup of coffee from Eli. The steam rising off the coffee carried the scent of the fresh coffee with it and Sid breathed deep of the aroma, blowing a little on the hot java before daring to take his first sip. He looked up from his cup and saw the patch of black beside Eli, frowned, and leaned forward to see better. He looked up at Eli, "Uh, that belong to you?" nodding to the wolf pup.

Eli chuckled, "Yeah, he adopted me a while back, been followin' all the way, so I guess we done buddied up, like it or not. Answers to Lobo, sometimes."

Sid looked at Eli, back to the pup, and shook his head, "Never thought I'd see the day..."

After Sid left, Eli and Lobo started for the trees to find a trail to the crest of the ridge and the point of the hill beyond. A narrow game trail that was well used started to the crest, but bent to sidle along the ridge, away from Eli's chosen promontory. He cut through the thick woods, stepping over downed snags, pushing through the thickets, and making the steep climb to the crest. He broke from the trees near the summit and moved to the top in a crouch. He bellied down and slipped the binoculars from the case and began his survey of the wild country below.

He did not expect to see smoke at this time of day, and with the timber so thick, he was doubtful he would see anything else that would be a giveaway, but he had to try. He focused on the break in the timber that marked where the road cut through and followed it, the trees giving away to show a break in the thick woods, a clearing that was suitable for a camp or the break in the terrain marked by a steep rockfall or more. As he moved the glasses, the glimmer of movement caught his eye and he focused on the area, spotted the loose horses that trotted along a trail that sided the road. He grinned, knowing the herd animals were looking for others of their herd and were following where the outlaws had traveled.

The trail dropped over a ridge and out of sight, but it told Eli that the outlaws were at least that far down the trail and probably further. He kept his glasses on the basin beyond, seeing a clearing with a pond, and saw the horses come from the timber and stop at the water. Eli scanned the area beyond, seeing nothing, but knew the outlaws would not be too much further if they were going to make a try for the wagons. It was the way of evil, always wanting to do their dastardly deeds out of sight and under cover and away from the eyes of judgmental men. He was reminded of the scripture in John, *...and men loved darkness rather than light, because their deeds were evil For every one that doeth evil hateth the light, neither cometh to the light, lest his deeds should be reproved.*

With one last scan, Eli rose and started back to his camp, Lobo trotting beside. He thought he would have a good meal, some coffee, and start back on the trail. Maybe he could find their camp before dark, if not, maybe later.

# CHAPTER 27

## DISCOVERY

The Naches Pass road, once it dropped over the crest, moved westerly along the stretch of the flat-top ridge that stood above the headwaters of the Greenwater River. Off his left shoulder in the far distance, the hoary head of Mount Rainier stood with its wintry cape of white showing a hint of pink from the slow-setting sun. Old Sol shone bright in his face, but Eli dipped his head, letting the brim of his felt hat shade his eyes, as he watched the trail and the thick trees nearby. He was on a game trail that paralleled the road and had probably been the original Naches Pass trail before the settlers did their best by clearing the tall timber, leaving rotting stumps and deadfall in their wake, all to make it easier for misplaced settlers to cross the forbidding Cascade mountains.

The road made a couple of switchbacks as it dropped over the big shoulder of the broad ridge, then sided a lower ridge that was pointed to the west. When it rounded the point, Eli saw the steep slope that Sid had mentioned. Eli moved into the trees, tethered the horses, and with binoculars in hand, he found an outcropping of rock that overhung a steep basaltic cliff, and dropped to his haunches for another look-see before he lost the sunlight. The Greenwater River, more of a creek at this stage, chuckled over the cascades close to a thousand feet below. On the far side of this ridge, another smaller creek twisted its way from the high country, to merge with the Greenwater off the point of this ridge. It was there, in the gulch that carried the no-name creek, a thin tendril of smoke rose from the trees.

He focused in on the shadowy timber, saw movement that told of tethered horses, then plotted his approach to the camp. He had to get a better idea of what they were planning, whether they had tucked tail and run, or were they waiting for the freighters and the gold that they probably knew about. Eli thought back to his battle with the brigands that resulted in several of them crossing over the great divide to meet their Maker and tried to picture each one of the dead. He knew the leader of the bunch had taken two bullets in the chest just before the fire raged over his body, but what about the one he had been arguing with, Wally Ainsley?

The camp was about a half-mile below and with a glance over his shoulder to where the horses were tethered, another look to the camp, he knew he had to go closer. He returned to the horses, loosened the girths on the saddles, slipped the Colt revolver shotgun from the pack and slipped the sling over his shoulder, checked the loads on both revolvers, touched the haft of the knife for reassurance, and with a glance back to the horses, another glance to the darkening sky, he started through the timber.

As the sun turned off its light, the stars began to light their lanterns and the moon, waxing to half, smiled from the eastern sky, but it was not high enough to be any help to Eli. He squinted as he carefully felt his way through the shadowy darkness, but his presence did not alarm any of the night creatures that welcomed the night with their harmony of sounds. Crickets began their rattling cacophony, a squirrel sounded the last of his chattering scolds, and a lonesome coyote sent his barking cough to the stars, hoping for a romantic interlude with another.

His night vision sharpened, and his steps stretched, yet Eli was still cautious as he felt every step beneath the leather of his moccasins. The smell of smoke kept him oriented until he heard the voices of men, growling and griping at one another. Eli shook his head, knowing the way of evil men that continually fought for leadership or at least to have their ideas accepted. The prominent voice was familiar and as Eli moved to a big ponderosa near the edge of their camp, he stood and listened.

"I'm tellin' ya what we knew 'fore that bunch jumped our camp an' durn nigh kilt ever'body! Silas had him a plan, shore, but we ain't got the men to do it! Now, here's what I'm tellin' we gots to do to take them wagons wit' just the five of us. First off, we'll ride back up the trail a spell, picket them hosses, an' make our approach through the trees. Lucas, you'n Jubal thar will move 'roun back o' the wagons careful like, an' cut the throat of any o' them teamsters sleepin' unner the wagons an' such. Jeb, you'n Art thar, you'll come at 'em slow like from the openin' o' thar circle, guns ready, but usin' yore knives is best."

"An' what'll you be doin', Wally," asked Lucas, scowling at the man as they sat circled around the low fire. Eli grinned as he watched, knowing when a man stares into a fire, or is near a fire, his night vision is worthless.

"I'll be o'erseein' what'chu fellas is doin' and watchin' fer anybody sneakin' up on you! Don'tchu know thar's allus gotta be somebody seein' the whole pit'cher?" growled Wally. He stood and turned to look back toward the tethered horses, giving Eli a look at his middle where the pistol and sword showed him to be the same man he had spotted before his first attack on their camp. The slovenly Wally spat a stream of tobacco juice at the fire, causing it to sizzle and flare, making the others lean back away, and scowl at their self-appointed leader.

"Now, let's get us a little shut-eye an' give them teamsters time to fall asleep. We'll move out in 'bout a hour," ordered Wally.

Eli had already started to the picket line of their horses, before Wally ordered the men to get some sleep. Picking his way to the animals, talking low and moving slow, he approached with an outstretched hand, glancing back to the camp, and approached the first horse, reaching out to stroke his face and neck as he slipped the halter over the ears of the horse. The animal dipped and shook his head, glad to be free of the halter, but watched as Eli did the same with the other horses. The animals were a little restless, but his calm voice kept them near.

Eli turned back into the trees, slipping his shotgun from his shoulder and holding it before him. He approached the camp silently until he was near and directly behind Wally. He leaned his head back slightly, took a deep breath, and let out the most hideous and loud scream he could concoct. He lifted the Colt as the men jumped and looked into the darkness to see a flame stab the night and the shotgun roar as it blasted the entire group with a hail of lead pellets, sparing not a one. As they staggered back from the blast, Eli started walking toward them, screaming and shooting, again and again. Wally staggered back, grabbing at his middle for his weapons, and fell into the fire, the flames showing a face of bloody pulp as he squirmed and screamed a wail that matched that of his attacker, Eli.

Lucas had stood and took the brunt of a full blast, stumbling back into Jubal who was also bloodied, and both men fell on their backs, Lucas's arm flailing into the fire, but he was dead as the flames licked at his whiskery and bloody face. The next blast took Art and Jeb, but Art had turned away, searching the darkness for his rifle. He bent to pick it up just as the Colt roared and he took the buckshot in the side and hip, but Jeb was facing full-on and took the rest of the shot in his face, driving him back on his heels.

The shotgun was empty, and Eli tossed it aside and kept walking toward the fire, grabbing for his Colt pistol on his hip and the LeMat pistol at his back. Both hands came around spitting fire as Eli continued his screaming and shooting. Art had fallen forward, twisted around with his rifle in hand, but the first shot from Eli's Colt took him in the chest and split his sternum, driving through his chest to tear apart his spine. Jeb was backpedaling, but not fast enough to escape the lead spat by the Colt and his chest blossomed red as he dropped to his knees, sightless eyes staring at the fire before he fell on his face.

The LeMat pistol barked, stabbing flame into the darkness beyond the circle of fire, catching Jubal as he was crabbing back away from the others, eyes so wide and full of fear they showed like lanterns reflecting the fire, but when the LeMat silenced, Jubal had stopped moving, eyes staring at the stars and unmoving.

The stench of burning flesh lifted from the fire, and Eli turned away, but looked back and had a better thought. With his neckerchief over his nose and mouth, he retrieved his Colt shotgun, stood it against a tree, and grabbed up as much scattered dead wood, limbs, and more as he could find and piled it on the fire, spreading the flames to consume the bodies of all the men. He went where the horses had been picketed and saw only darkness. The melee from the shooting had forced the animals to scatter into the woods. He had no interest in the packs and gear of the outlaws, thinking that if the gear was like the men, it was probably infested with ticks, lice, and hardbacks. Eli grinned, shook his head, retrieved the shotgun, and started back to his own horses.

He made a camp in the trees above the road, knowing the approach of the wagons as they started the steep descent to the bottom, would be enough to wake him, if he wasn't awake already. But it had been a busy night and he needed some sleep. The horses stood quiet as Eli took to his blankets, only to find orange eyes beside them, and the wolf pup waiting for him. Eli grinned, stretched out, and was soon asleep.

# Chapter 28

# Green River

Eli watched as the morning sun painted the tips of the peaks to the north. He sat in the shadow of tall fir trees that crested the long ridge that rose above the descending road of the Naches Trail. He had his time with the Lord and flipped open the pages of his Bible to resume his reading in the book of Isaiah, chapter 41. He grinned as he read verse 19, *I will set in the desert the fir tree, and the pine, and the box tree together: That they may see, and know, and consider, and understand together, that the hand of the Lord hath done this, and the Holy One of Israel hath created it.*

Eli lifted his eyes to the wonder of God's creation all around him. The granite-tipped peaks that lifted their bald heads above the dark green carpet of pines and firs and spruce, the deep valleys that had yet to feel the warmth of morning light but carried the spring runoff of winter's snows, cascading over the rocks with a melody of the wild. Even the scars that cut through the mountains and forests that were made by the advance of man held a certain poetry of design and told the tale of man fulfilling his destiny.

A nudge from a cold nose at his hip split Eli's face with a smile as he looked down and stroked the warm fur of the wolf pup. Lifting his binoculars, he began his morning scan of the valley that held the decimated camp of the would-be outlaws and raiders, moved his search down the valley bottom to the point of the ridge he sat upon, and brought it back along the road below that hung on the edge of the cliff and talus slope that dropped into the valley of the Greenwater River. There was no sign of men, friendly or otherwise, but the creatures of the forest were making their way to the streams for their morning refreshment. He saw a handful of cow elk trailing their orange-coated calves on the upper reaches of the no-name creek. On the Greenwater headwaters, a small band of bighorn sheep were led by the always watchful boss ram to split the willows for their morning drink. Further downstream some mule deer went to a familiar spot where they always took their water.

With rifle in hand, the field glasses in the case hanging from his shoulder, and with the little shadow of a wolf at his heels, Eli started back through the trees to return to his camp and make some coffee. The little shoulder that held his camp was above the road, but shrouded by the trees, yet offered Eli a glimpse of the road and anything that moved. He sat back on the log, elbows on knees as he watched the coffeepot begin its dance at the edge of the little fire that also held the frying pan with some smoked meat warming and the last of his cornmeal biscuits that sat atop, soaking up any excess grease.

He was finishing his meal and lifting his cup for a drink of java when he heard the first of the trace chains and the crack of the teamster's whip. He stood and craned around to look through the trees to see Sid leading the wagons to the bend around the point before they would start the steeper descent to the bottom. Eli walked through the trees and hailed Sid as he approached and continued sipping his coffee and chewing on the smoked meat and cornmeal sandwich. Sid signaled the wagons to stop and nudged his mount closer to Eli.

"Whatsamatta, lose your horses?" he grinned, leaning forward to rest an elbow on the pommel.

"Oh, just havin' a little breakfast while I wait on you," replied a grinning Eli.

"Any trouble?" asked Sid, frowning and looking about.

"Oh, I had to have a little talk with the rest o' them raiders 'fore they came to an understanding. But there won't be any more trouble from that bunch."

"Good, good. We're gonna hold up here, make us some Mormon brakes, then we'll go on down the hill yonder. Maybe after you finish your breakfast, you can scout on ahead?" suggested Sid.

"Sure, sure. I'll do that. How far you think you'll make it today?"

Sid huffed, shaking his head, "We'll be lucky to get all the wagons down this hill today. But once we've done that, the worst will be behind us, and we can make better time. The road follows the Greenwater and the White Rivers and the land gets purty level, so..." he shrugged.

"So, you might not be needin' a scout the rest of the way?" inquired Eli.

"You're welcome to stay with us till we get to Fort Steilacoom if'n you want. Your providin' us with fresh meat is always welcome."

"Well, I been thinkin' 'bout muh boys, wonderin' if that riverboat'll be comin' back upriver," drawled Eli, lifting his glazed eyes to the distant mountains, his mind bringing the images of his sons to the fore. He stood silent for a moment as he reminisced, but was brought back when Sid said, "Well, if you don't wanna scout, you can always cut us some timbers for them brakes."

Eli grinned, "Me? I ain't no lumberjack!" and laughed as he turned to return to his camp and ready his animals for the day's scout.

————

HE BROKE through the trees and sat aboard Rusty as he reined up near the first of the wagons. He watched as the men, having fashioned the first of the brakes, were packing rocks to fill in the middle. Shaped like a triangle about six feet wide at the base and with the point to the wagon, the logs were secured together at the points with long dowels and spikes. A chain from the point to the undercarriage of the wagon would drag the rock-filled brake behind, keeping the wagon from descending the steep roadway too fast, forcing the mules to dig in to pull the braked wagon downhill. This part of the road had been reworked and carved across the face of the hills to replace the original route that required the wagons to be lowered by ropes and chains down the face of the steep hill. Although still precarious, it was much safer and easier to traverse than the original route used a decade past.

Eli moved aside to let the first braked wagon pass and followed well behind to avoid the dust cloud that trailed the wagon. He grinned at the ingenuity of man, chuckled at the persistence of determined travelers and explorers, and cut through the trees to follow a narrow game trail to the bottom.

It was early afternoon after following the meandering Greenwater River through the timbered hills, that Eli broke into the flats at the confluence of the Greenwater and White Rivers. After the Greenwater pushed past a long ridge in the widening valley, the two rivers paralleled one another for about two miles, although separated by a span of thick timber about a mile wide, before converging below the face of a big foothill that marked the end of the wide valley and forced the White River to the west to find its way to the distant flatlands.

He spotted a stretch of sandy shoals and riverbank between the road and the river and pushed the big stallion through the narrow line of trees to let both horses get a good drink as he knelt beside the river to scoop up some water for himself. The river made a sharp bend to the west where a small creek came from the hills to the north and emptied its meager stream into the bigger river. Eli stood, stretched, and looked at the hills to the northwest where a big mountain stretched about two thousand feet higher, lifting its black timber to stand as the barrier to the north. The valley to the east of the tall peak dropped steeply between the two tall hills that were the last of the foothills that lay in the shadow of the taller mountains behind them.

With an unquenched thirst for hot coffee, Eli loosened the girths on the horses, picketed them at the edge of the willows and the grassy flat, and began gathering up some dry grey driftwood that had been deposited at high water level in the spring runoff. He soon had his fire going and another pot of coffee dancing as he gnawed on some smoked meat, tossing Lobo his share of the feast.

The clatter of hooves and the shuffling gait in the

dusty trail warned Eli of riders approaching. He nudged Rusty into the thicker trees, well away from the trail but within sight. He stepped down, stroked the muzzle of the big stallion, and pulled the grey closer to keep them both quiet when he spotted the movement on the trail. Two men, both trailing heavily laden packhorses, were riding eastbound on the trail above. They were slumped in their saddles, heads hanging, lulled into a snooze by the steady rocking gait of their horses. The visible gear on the packs, big pans, shovels, picks, and more, told Eli these were wannabe prospectors, probably bound for the goldfields of Montana Territory. The newer strikes in Bear Gulch country had attracted many of the forty-niners from California; men that had little luck in the goldfields that had been mined out in the far west were following the siren call of riches to the high country.

Eli grinned as the riders shuffled past, totally unaware of his presence, caring little for his disdain of their endless hopes and pursuits. He slipped his watch from his vest pocket and decided to keep on the trail. As he mounted Rusty, he looked through the towering tree-tops to see the lowering sun and guessed he had about another two or three hours of daylight to make some time, maybe get some fresh meat for the teamsters.

## CHAPTER 29

# NORTHWEST

These were the historic lands of the Puyallup, Muckleshoot, Nisqually, Cowlitz, and other Northwestern peoples. Eli had been two days on the trail that sided the White River when the river and road passed between two pyramid peaks blanketed in thick black timber and broke into the open to see the wide flats before him. He nudged Rusty into the trees that skirted the lower rises of the butte on the north side of the road. A clearing, just inside the trees but out of sight of the trail, showed signs of many campers before— a fire ring, poles between trees for shelters, trodden down space among the trees that had been used to corral animals, and more. Eli grinned at the signs of settlers that scarred the land and changed their surroundings forever.

He settled into the camp, started his gather of firewood, most broken and dead limbs from the nearby trees that he broke off and piled close by. Satisfied with the makings of his camp, he took rifle in hand, binoculars in the case, and with a wave to Lobo, started his climb to the shoulder of the butte for his customary survey of the territory. Choosing the point of a shoulder where the timber thinned, he leaned the rifle against the trunk of a nearby tree, went to the break in the trees, and lifted the binoculars. Stretching out to the northwest, the White River with its many cottonwoods and more that always hugged the waterways, disappeared in the hazy distance. Eli recognized the familiar haze of big waters, knowing the south end of Puget Sound lay in that direction.

Sid had told him that from this point on to Fort Steilacoom would be another two days, but that would also mark the end of the journey for the freighters. As he scanned the flats, he saw several farms, some open land, roads, and all the other signs of civilization that he had come to resent. He grinned as he thought of his change of ways and how he had become such an isolationist and outdoorsman, annoyed of the crowds of settlers that were doing as their name implied, settling the land, turning wilderness into farms and ranches, towns and stores, and attracting even more people.

He was at least a day ahead of the freighters and was considering whether to go on to Fort Steilacoom or to return to Walla Walla in hopes of seeing his boys return from their work on the riverboat. His mind wandered back to Wallula and the riverboats, hoping the twins would return and he would have the opportunity to see them again and bring them up to date about their mother and the family farm and more. They were named in the will of their mother's family and would inherit the horse farm. But he also knew they had shown little interest in the family operation, their eyes were always set on life in the west and making their own fortunes.

He stood, stretched, and looked around, just enjoying the views and the smells of the mountains. *I like the*

*Cascades, bigger trees, amazing view, but there's something about the Rockies that seem to have a pull on me.* With another look about, he started back through the trees to return to camp and fix his supper, the coffeepot was calling, and he had to respond. With Lobo at his heels, he moved through the tall trees, retracing his steps on the dim game trail. But as he neared the camp, he was surprised to smell coffee. He had not started his fire, nor put the coffee on, yet there was no mistaking the smell of coffee for a man that was hankering a cup. He paused, slipped the rifle from his shoulder, and cautiously moved through the last of the trees. Sitting on the grey log was a man, his back to Eli, and a portly woman moving about the fire, tending to the steaks hanging over the flames, and something cooking in the frying pan. He caught a whiff of the corn dodgers in the pan and started into the open. "Evenin', folks," he lowered his rifle and continued his approach as if they were old friends. "Smells good!"

He went to the log and sat down, lay the rifle against the log, and sat the binocular case beside his left foot. He turned to the man, extended his hand to shake, "I'm Eli, Eli McCain," and stretched to offer his hand to the man who was a big man, stoic expression, black braids hanging to his shoulders from under his hat that had a long feather in the band. The broad-shouldered man appeared to be about the same age as Eli, but a little bigger. The visitor turned, expressionless, accepted the offered hand, "I am Black Bear Williams, this is my woman, Miriam. We are of the Buklshuhls, or Muckleshoot people. We have been following you since you left our land of the Greenwater and White Rivers."

When Lobo came around the end of the log and lay beside Eli's foot, Black Bear pulled away slightly and looked from the wolf to the man and back. Without a word, he accepted the cup of coffee offered by his woman, watched as she poured a cup for Eli, and with a slight shake of his head, he mumbled, "White men," and sipped his coffee.

Eli looked at Black Bear, "Why were you following me?"

Black Bear sipped his coffee, looked into the flames of the fire, "After the war between our people and yours, we were sent to the reservation. It is a small place in the wetlands," he nodded to the west, "but our land had always been in the mountains, along the White River where the Greenwater joins. We," he lifted his eyes to his woman, "ride to the mountains when we can, for we need to breathe the air of the pines and feel the breeze of the mountains. If we do not do this, we do not feel alive. It is in our land that we hunt and bring home the meat we like."

He sipped some more coffee and continued, "There were many of the people of these lands, the Nisqually, Puyallup, Klickitat, and our Muckleshoot, that were led by the Nisqually chief, Leschi. But the white men were too many, and now we must live on the reservation." He leaned back, finished his coffee, and grinned, "But we can leave when we want, to go hunting and fishing. When the salmon run, we all come to the land of our people to take the fish for our winter."

He looked to Eli, "We followed you because you were in our land, and we know what you did to the men who were fouling our land with their presence and the way they were with their animals. You did what I wanted to do, but could not, because I am Native."

Eli grinned, "Those men and others planned to attack the freight wagon train that I was scouting for and had attacked another wagon train of settlers, killed them all, women and children and I had to stop them."

"You have done well. We need more men like you," interjected his woman, Miriam, handing him a filled plate with the meat and more that she had prepared.

Eli nodded, smiled, "Thank you."

She chuckled. "It is your food." She grinned, and turned to prepare a plate for her man.

―――――

ELI ROSE EARLY and went with Lobo to the high point shoulder of the pyramid hill for his morning time with his Lord. The visitors were stirring about in the camp when he left, but his time on the mountain was more important to him. It was shaping up to be another beautiful day with a clear sky, cool breezes, and the birds sang their songs to serenade the visitor to their realm. After his morning reverie, he returned to camp to a surprise breakfast prepared by Miriam. She had gone to the river's edge and harvested several duck eggs and had the pork belly sizzling and was preparing to fry the eggs. She smiled up at Eli, and he said, "This could easily get to be a habit! I'm not used to having good meals prepared by a good woman!"

Miriam smiled a timid and embarrassed smile but continued tending the food with a quick glance to Eli. She asked, "Are you staying in this camp long?"

"The freighters that I've been scouting for should be here today. I'll wait for them, but I'm thinking about returning over the mountains to Wallula. I have twin sons that work on one of the riverboats and I'm hoping to see them when they return."

"We have a son and a daughter. They have their own

families and are on the reservation. They do not go to the mountains like we do. My son and the husband of our daughter work for a white man boat builder and have lost the ways of their ancestors." She dropped her eyes, obviously disappointed in her offspring, but enjoying her life with her man. "We will return to our home on the reservation today."

It was late morning when the sounds of the freighters alerted Eli to the coming of the wagon train. His visitors had been gone for a couple hours and he had cleared his camp, ready to depart. He walked down to the road and hailed Sid as he neared. When Sid reined up and leaned on his pommel, he asked, "So, we have not had any more trouble. You?"

"Nah, the last of that bunch with the horses, is the last of that bunch," answered Eli.

"So, you stayin' or goin'?" asked Sid, seeing the look of wanderlust in Eli's eyes.

Eli chuckled, "Goin'. Thought I might get back to Walla Walla in time to see muh boys."

"Understand. Thanks for your scoutin' an' such. Much appreciated." He leaned back and pulled a pouch from his belt and counted out several double eagle gold pieces and leaned over to hand them to Eli. "Anytime we're both in the same place, you can ride with me. Like the old-timers used to say, you'll do to ride the river with."

# CHAPTER 30

## CASCADES

The smooth gait of the long-legged stallion often allowed Eli to slip into a time of reverie. Always vigilant on the trail, his mind surrendered to his reflections and his hopes. His hand lay lightly on the pommel, the reins looped through his fingers, images of the past and envisioned hopes danced through his mind, interlacing themselves into a quilt of opportunities missed and uncertain possibilities. When minds are allowed to wander unhindered, accusations and recriminations often fill the void with guilt and despair, but Eli knew when his thoughts were directed by the Scripture, God washes our minds clean and fills it with his comfort and guidance. Several scriptures came to mind; *For as he thinketh in his heart, so is he. Proverbs 23:7, Fear thou not; for I am with thee: be not dismayed; for I am thy God: I will strengthen thee; yea, I will help thee; yea, I will uphold thee with the right hand of my righteousness. Isaiah 41:10.*

Eli knew in his heart he had to trust what the Lord was doing in his life, but at times it seemed He was assaulted with the troubles of others and forced into their lives to help them. He had always been a man that refused to turn a blind eye or deaf ear to others that were in despair, often reminded of his father that lived a life that was the picture of what many called the golden rule —*Do unto others as you would have them do unto you.* The words of his father came back to him, words that he had often repeated to his growing, awkward, and curious sons, but the words were from the book of Jeremiah 29:11, *For I know the thoughts that I think toward you, saith the Lord, thoughts of peace, and not of evil, to give you an expected end. Then shall ye call upon me, and ye shall go and pray unto me, and I will hearken unto you. And ye shall seek me, and find me, when ye shall search for me with all your heart.* Eli muttered the thoughts aloud, "Lord, I trust you to give me that 'expected end' and I know my father said that 'expected end' meant you would give me both a future and a hope, but it sure would be nice if I could know what that future was gonna be!"

The sudden stop of Rusty brought Eli back to the present with a start. Rusty's head was lifted, his ears pricked, and the grey had stepped alongside to look toward the trees. He, too, stood with ears pricked and nostrils flaring. There was no noise, the usual sounds of the day had silenced until the snarl and spit of a cata-mount made the horses skittish and sidestep. Eli snatched his Spencer from the scabbard by his left knee and swung to the ground, dropping the reins to ground tie the big stallion. He knew the grey would stay beside the claybank. Eli stroked the neck of Rusty, speaking assurances quietly as he stepped before the big stallion and started toward the trees.

The thick timber shielded what he knew was a cougar, but he was hopeful the cat of the mountains was feasting on a kill and not interested in any others. Again came the snarl, cough, and spit and Eli moved closer, the Spencer held before him, hammer cocked and ready. As he leaned to the side to see past the big red cedar he saw the mountain lion, cornered by four big grey wolves that had formed a semicircle in their attempt to drive the cougar off the bloody carcass of a black-tailed deer. The wolves were in their attack stance, heads lowered, teeth showing as they snarled their warnings to the big cat. As if on cue, the four took a short step forward, but the big cat snarled and feinted a lunge, made a swipe at the air with claws extended as if to warn the wolves what those talons could do, causing the four to flinch but not leave. Eli watched the confrontation for a few seconds more until one of the wolves decided he was not as hungry as he thought and stepped back, eyes on the cougar, another step, then he turned and trotted into the trees. His movement prompted the other wolves to follow, and the cat relaxed, sat back on his haunches, and tore a big strip of meat from the side of the deer and bellied down to enjoy his feast.

Eli chuckled, started backstepping until he was behind the cover of several big trees, then relaxed and returned to the horses. He spoke softly as he approached, stroked both horses' muzzles and necks, then swung aboard Rusty and with a gentle leg pressure, they started on the trail again, with the horses often craning around to look fearfully at the trees but they stepped up their gait and soon put the smell of cougar behind them.

It was early afternoon when they reached the confluence of the Greenwater and White Rivers and Rusty bent his head around to look at Eli as if asking when he was going to stop. With a chuckle and a nudge, they moved through the willows at the river's edge and stopped for a long drink. Eli stepped down, loosened the girths, and began gathering some firewood for his coffee making.

―――――

BY NIGHTFALL, he had mounted the steep descent on the face of the long ridge where he had camped after his last confrontation with the raiders. He gave the horses a good rubdown, made a quick camp, and after his meal, turned in for the night.

―――――

FOLLOWING his time on the hill for his prayer and vigil, he had the last of the coffee, put the leftover biscuits and meat in a bundle and into the saddlebags, and was soon on his way. By the fall of dusk, he passed the site of the wagon train massacre and continued downstream on the Little Naches to find a campsite. He wanted to make as much time as possible and hasten his return to Walla Walla to hopefully get some news about the riverboats and the return of his sons. Another day saw him at the pillar of basalt on the south end of a bend in the river and he knew he was nearing the mouth of the long canyon and the open flats beyond. The greenery of the high mountains had given way to the dusky shades of brown with the sage-brush, bunchgrasses, and cacti that painted the hillsides.

Late afternoon the following day saw him riding past the flat mesa with its basaltic rimrock and soon came to the confluence of the Naches and Yakima Rivers. The trail turned south to split the foothills and open the valley of the Yakama Reservation and the land where

Moses Carpenter and his people were planning their homesteads.

The sound of axes thunking into hardwood and the rasp of two-man saws gnawing away at the trees told Eli the men were hard at work, felling trees and more, to build their cabins. He pushed Rusty across the waters of the Yakima River and through the willows and sat watching the shirtless men sweating and toiling in the coolness of late afternoon. One of the men looked up, grinned, and hailed Eli, motioning him to come near. It was easy to recognize the big framed and heavily muscled Moses Carpenter, the former Sergeant Major Carpenter, that had served with him during the latter years of the Civil War.

Eli slipped to the ground and grasped the sweaty hand of his grinning friend and drew him close for a wet bear hug, but the two old friends minded not that the result of hard labor had put a shine on the ebony skin of one and not the other. They laughed and chided one another until Moses motioned to the shade and a big rock for them to be seated and catch up.

"I see you made it back all in one piece! Did you have any trouble?" asked Moses as he wiped his brow and neck, looking sidelong at his friend.

"Let's just say I didn't get bored," drawled Eli, grinning.

"That bad, huh?" replied Moses, his countenance going stoic. "Bad as Appomattox?"

Eli huffed, "Ain't nuthin' ever gonna be as bad as that! But it was interesting."

"Sid had 'nuff guns then?"

"I don't think they ever fired a shot," resolved Eli. They continued mulling over the trip for a few moments, until Eli asked, "Makin' progress with your cabins?"

A broad grin split Moses's face as a deep rumbling laugh that shook his frame came rolling out between them. "Colonel, we have the prettiest little farm you could ever ask for, rich land, good water, shade trees, and a perfect spot for Mama's cabin on top of a little rise where she can see me plowin' the field as she sits on the porch givin' instructions!"

Eli chuckled, "No trouble with the Yakama?"

"They eben been he'pin'! Best folks you could find for neighbors, even brought us some seed an' more."

"And the rest of the families?"

"All doin' well, happy as a tree full o' larks, yessir. Men're busy, women workin', anxious to set up house keepin', Abigail Harrison showin' she's gonna have 'nother'n. Had church an' most'a the Natives came, had more red'ns than black'ns," he chuckled, his big chest rising and falling as he thought of their many friends among the Yakama.

He sobered as he turned to look at Eli, "Any word on your boys?"

"No, but I'm hopin' I'll hear somethin' when I get back to Walla Walla."

Moses grinned, "An' what about you'n Miss Kennedy?" he chuckled.

Eli grinned, "No plans that direction. I had my time with a wife, now my feelings are full of these mountains," nodding to the west and the Cascades, back to the east and the Rockies.

"They shore is pretty, ain't they?" drawled Moses, grinning broadly and nodding as he looked to the mountains with their quilt work of snow and granite that stood above timberline. He turned to look directly at Eli, "You're stayin' fer supper! Ethel and Lucas'll be anxious to see you, an' if'n I don' bring you home, she'll strip the hide right off'n me!"

Eli grinned, "There's nothing I'd like better than to join your family and have one of Ethel's home-cooked meals!" declared Eli, laughing.

# CHAPTER 31

# WALLULA

His mackintosh had been at the bottom of the pannier, but Eli had wasted no time digging it out and slipping it over his shoulders. After the continued rumble of thunder that he felt as well as heard, and the skeletal fingers of lightning that walked across the flats, he knew he was in for a gulley washer. When the deluge came, he was in the open, had been for two days, and the horses' heads hung as the water dripped off their manes. Eli kept looking for shelter, but the hillsides were devoid of any overhangs, tree clusters, anything that might offer an escape from the downpour, and they plodded on to the southeast, siding the Yakima River and its scattered willows, scrawny cottonwoods, and cascading waters.

The water was coming from atop the wide plateau that stood above the Yakima Valley, catching the deluge in its wide-stretched arms and funneling it into the ravines and gullies to send it crashing and splashing to the Yakima River and on to the Columbia. But the muddy waters that came from the plateau were carving their new paths down the face of the hillsides that had seen little water this summer, pushing and churning their way, carrying debris, mud, and more to the bottom. The big stallion plodded along the muddy trail, each footfall going a little deeper in the mud, each hoof heavier with the adobe mix clinging and building on its hooves, making the trek harder with every step.

The hillsides shouldered in, forcing the road between the hills and the river, closer to the raging waters, but the river made a sharp bend to the north, away from the trail, and disappeared into the sheets of rain. A cluster of tall cottonwoods sided by alders beckoned and Eli nudged the big horse toward the trees. There was a bit of shelter offered in the thick trees, leafy limbs hanging but shedding the worst of the rain, and a grassy patch that lay under the wide limbs, water dripping away. Eli reined up, slipped to the ground, and led the horses into the shelter, taking the driest spot for himself, yet stripped the gear from the animals and picketed them near with enough lead line to let them wander if they chose, but not enough for them to get away.

He sat down at the base of the trunk, leaned back against the rough bark, and relaxed. A drenched Lobo shook and rolled his hide to rid himself of excess water and stretched out next to Eli. It was not dry, but it was drier. He kept his mackintosh tight, his hat on, and glanced at the horses, relaxed, and let the lessening rain lull him to sleep.

The rain let up and he pushed on toward the crossing of the Columbia River. With a glance to the sun that was doing its best to come out of hiding, he guessed he would make his night camp on this side of the river, and after crossing, would have a long day's travel to make it to Walla Walla. He found himself looking forward to seeing Donna and finding out how she was doing with her new venture in the restaurant business. He shook his head as he thought of spending time with a woman, but he definitely enjoyed her cooking.

He lifted his face to the warmth of the sun that was pushing away the dark clouds of the storm and beginning to bathe the countryside in bright sunshine, a welcome respite after the cloudburst. Even the horses were moving with a brisk step, especially since they left the trail and were moving through the grassy flats, avoiding the adobe clay mud of the trail. It would dry soon enough, but in its wet state, it was a thick, gooey mess that clung to anything and everything. Even wagons could not travel in the muck.

When he came within sight of the Columbia River, the sun had warmed the land and the roads and fields were drying. A cluster of trees at the foot of the rolling hills that backed up the butte with the basaltic cliffs facing the river offered Eli a campsite for the night. He nudged the horses through the trees to the well-used campsite and stepped down. He stripped the gear from the horses, let them roll, and led them to water. He gave them both a good rubdown, picketed them, and started making his camp. He was hungry for a good meal and some hot coffee, and he busied himself preparing the makings.

A hail from beyond the trees moved Eli to his weapons stacked on the gear, and he answered the call with a "C'mon in, if you're friendly. Keep your hands clear and we'll talk."

Two men, a woman, and a pair of heavy laden pack-horses pushed through the trees as Eli watched. The man in the lead, clean-shaven, well set up, leaned on his pommel, "Mind if we share the camp? We've got vittles aplenty an' muh wife's a good cook!"

Eli grinned, "I've never been known to turn down a woman-cooked meal. Step on down."

The man grinned, turned and nodded to his companions, and stepped to the ground. He moved toward Eli, hand outstretched, "I'm Michael Farmer, this," nodding to the woman, "is muh wife, Kerri. And that," pointing to the other man, "is muh brother, Miles. We're headin' up the Naches, goin' to Fort Steilacoom."

"Just came from there," replied Eli, accepting the man's hand and shaking as he added, "My name's Eli, Eli McCain." He gathered an armload of firewood and dropped it by the fire ring and set about getting the fire started, while the men tended their horses.

Farmer stopped, looked at Eli, "You just came from there? I thought you was makin' camp an' headin' to the mountains."

"Nope, headin' back to Walla Walla. This your first time o'er the pass?" asked Eli.

"Yup. We been in Montana Territory, an' we're gonna have a look-see at the land this side o' the fort, decide whether we wanna make a home there, or go down the coast to California country," explained Michael. He was fetching some cooking utensils from the panniers that he had taken from the first packhorse for his wife. As they spoke, he and his brother were tending the horses and the gear but getting whatever his wife needed for making the meal.

Eli had filled a coffeepot with fresh water and sat it beside the fire, returned to the packs for some coffee and smoked meat. Kerri had set up a tripod over the fire and hung a big pot for the making of a stew. While she worked to prepare the meal, the men were busy setting up their camp, using long branches to spread between the trees for making their shelters.

After their meal, the four sat around, asking Eli about the trail ahead and any anticipated problems. He told of the terrain, warned of possible encounters with Natives, but assured them most were friendly. He said nothing about the renegade raiders and encouraged them as to the route and good travel. "As long as you're not taking wagons, you should have no trouble. You will pass a few graves, a site of a recent attack on a wagon train, but that wasn't from Natives. There's a mass grave on a little knoll, marked with a cross, that's recent. Up top, there's a couple graves that are recent, but nothing to be concerned about." Eli saw the woman frowning and fidgeting, turned away from her and stood to go to the trees.

When he returned, the three looked at him and the woman began asking questions, "Do you know anything about the wagons that were attacked?"

"What do you mean?"

"Well," she paused, dropped her eyes, glanced to her husband, "we had some friends and family that left before us. They were planning on taking the Naches Trail, and they were in a group of five or six wagons. Several families, children, you know." She sighed heavily, lifted her eyes to Eli, "We, uh, I was wondering if that wagon train might be those of our friends."

Eli frowned, looked at the woman, and chose his words carefully, not wanting to upset her needlessly. "Ma'am, there wasn't much left to recognize, the wagons were burnt and such. What personal belongings I could find, I buried at the end of the remains of one wagon, the one that still had two wheels, although even they were burned beyond use."

"What about the people? Did you see any of them?"

After a long pause, Eli answered, "I saw all of them."

"Can you tell me about them?" she asked.

"I could, but you don't want to hear it. If they are your friends and family, it's best to remember them as you last saw them," explained Eli. He glanced to the men, back to the woman, and reached for the coffeepot for a refill.

Kerri fell silent as tears welled up in her eyes and trailed down her cheeks. She shook her head and dropped her face into her hands. Michael put his hand on her shoulder to comfort her, but it did little good. "It might not be them, Kerri," consoled Michael.

Eli glanced to the man, caught his eye, and slowly shook his head as if to say, "It was them."

They talked into the night with the Farmers sharing their ambitions and hopes for their future home where they could settle down and put their wandering days behind them. Michael had his own vision of their home, a big house with kids and grandkids running around, big fields with plentiful crops, good neighbors, and more. They shared with Eli about their success in the goldfields of Montana Territory and how that success was to be shared with their extended family that had taken the wagon train to the Puget Sound area and that they were going to scout for land to settle.

Eli told the tale of his search for the twins and his hopes of soon finding them, but as to his future, it was an open book. But the telling of his lack of plans for his future beyond his search, tugged at Eli's mind and heart for it was nothing he had really verbalized before, and an emptiness seemed to lend a touch of futility to his nostalgia.

They turned in for the night and come morning, Eli

made his way to the promontory for his time to greet both the rising sun and his Lord in prayer. When he returned to the camp, the trio of visitors were mounting up and bid him goodbye and good luck, and Eli returned the greeting to his new friends.

# CHAPTER 32

## MILL CREEK

Eli led the horses off the ferry, paused and looked about. There were no riverboats at the docks of Wallula, but there were crates, boxes, barrels, and more stacked on the wharf awaiting wagons to transport them to town to be distributed to the businesses or shipped by freighters over the mountains to the gold-fields. He mounted up, pointing Rusty east to Walla Walla and set an easy pace to make the twenty-five or so miles to Walla Walla.

He followed the road beside the Walla Walla River until its convergence with Pine Creek and the road continued east to cross over the Little Walla Walla and sided Mill Creek into the town. It was dusk when he rode past the Mill Creek Café where Donna Kennedy was the new proprietor, but he continued on to the Bon Ton Hotel, anxious for a bath and a comfortable bed. He stabled the horses at the livery, leaving the wolf pup with Rusty, stripped the gear and stashed the tack and packs in the tack room but carried the saddlebags, bedroll, and weapons to the hotel. Once he secured a room, he took a fresh set of clothes to the bathhouse and washed off the road grime, donned his clean duds and with a shave and haircut at the barber, who was getting ready to close but was happy for the extra business, he was ready for his long anticipated meal at the Mill Creek Café.

It was the tail end of the evening meal hour when Eli pushed through the door and stood looking around. A loud squeal came from the kitchen entry, and he turned to see Donna, rushing toward him, arms outstretched and ran into his arms. She wrapped him in a warm embrace and began kissing him with a fervor he had not felt since before war's end. When she leaned back, his arms still around her waist, she was smiling broadly, and said, "Oh, I'm so glad you're back! I was so worried about you! I am so happy to see you!"

Eli chuckled, looking around at the few remaining customers who were grinning at the display, and with more than a little embarrassment, he asked, "Got'ny thing to eat?"

Donna giggled, "Of course we do!" She pulled away, led him to a table near the kitchen entry, and said, "You just sit right there, and I'll bring you a feast!" She stood, hands on hips, smiling broadly, and said, "It is so good to see you!" and whirled around and disappeared into the kitchen.

The sizzling of a steak on a platter came from the kitchen carried by a smiling Donna; it was loaded with steak, potatoes, biscuits, and more. She set the plate before him, sat down beside him, and watched as he said a short prayer of thanks, grinned and picked up his utensils, and set about making short work of the feast. Before he finished, Donna jumped up and soon returned with a plate holding a three-inch-thick slice of steaming apple pie. Big eyes looked at the pie, and with nothing more than a glance to Donna, Eli moved the platter away, pulled the pie close, and began to enjoy every bite.

When he was finished, he sighed heavily, leaned back, and smiled at Donna, "That was marvelous!"

"Oh, I'm so glad you liked it!" she smiled, staring at him as if she was imprinting his image on her mind and heart. She leaned back, relaxed, "So, now what?"

"What do you mean?" asked Eli, afraid of where this conversation might lead.

"About your sons? Any word?"

Eli, relieved, leaned his elbows on the table, "No, nothing. There were no boats at the docks, so I'm hoping the boat they were on might return soon, so, I'll be staying around a while."

Donna let a slow smile and a mischievous glint in her eyes paint her face as she leaned forward, scooted a little closer to Eli, "So, I get the pleasure of your company a while longer, huh?"

"Not going anywhere. But I expect you to keep me abreast of any news you might hear."

"According to folks hereabouts, any boat that docks below, the crew comes into town to spend any downtime here, and that means most of the crews come into the café here. I'm sure I'll hear about any boats that come this way." She paused, taking in the nearness of Eli, and added, "While you were gone there were three boats that came in and I asked the men about your boys, but none knew anything."

"Thanks for that. I know the boats from here don't always go all the way to the mouth of the Columbia, the river in the canyon is too rough, the canyon too narrow, and they portage most of the freight to boats that come up from further downstream and return to the ports below." He sighed, leaned back, "But the way things have been going, if my boys know I'm here looking for 'em, they could do just about anything. I know they've got money, some from their goldfield work, some wages, and probably some money from their grandmother. So, they could give anything a try, you know, young men on a great adventure and discovering themselves."

Donna dropped her hand to cover Eli's, and asked, "I'll be closing up. Will you wait for me, and we can take a walk in the moonlight?"

Eli grinned, looked at her, and asked, "Moonlight? Tryin' to get all romantic on me?"

Donna giggled, leaned her shoulder against his, and said, "Is it working?"

———

DONNA TUCKED her arm through the crook of Eli's arm and pulled herself close as they ambled down the boardwalk of Walla Walla. Most of the businesses were closed but others lay rectangles of light on the boardwalk while the big moon hung high overhead. When they passed a saloon, the tin pan piano and off-key voices accompanied the raucous laughter and spilled out the open doorways. When they came to the end of the businesses, they crossed over and walked back on the far side.

Donna asked, "Eli, have you ever thought of settling down? You know, having a permanent home, family, and more?"

Eli grinned, gave the question a thoughtful moment, "I have not had a 'home' as you call it, since I left my boyhood home to go to West Point. Then the military sent me around the country, ultimately the war, and after that, the search for my boys. I really haven't given it much thought because it wasn't much of a possibility, but of late..." he shrugged, grinning as he pulled her arm closer with his.

She smiled, snuggled a little closer, and continued with her thought, "Well, you know, I've looked at a few places, homes, and I've been giving it some thought. Funny thing, though, every time I picture myself in a home, it's always with you!" She leaned her head on his shoulder as they walked. She was waiting for a response from him, but they walked in silence, just enjoying the time and the evening stroll.

————

ELI SAT at the table in the corner, enjoying his coffee after a big breakfast of pork belly, eggs, potatoes, strip steak, and biscuits and gravy. Donna was pleased with his presence and made several forays from the kitchen, just to see him, although she busied herself tending the many patrons. While he sat savoring the moment, three men pushed through the door, a little raucous in their manner, but their attire and talk revealing they were from a recently docked riverboat. After they had been served and were waiting for their meal, Eli rose and stepped beside their table. "Excuse me, men, I couldn't help but overhear. I take it you're with a riverboat docked below?"

The men scowled at Eli, but one man answered, "That's right."

"If you don't mind, I'd like to ask you a question," as he spoke, he pulled the tintype from his pocket and held it to the speaker, "Those are my sons, twins, and I've been looking for them. They were said to have taken a job on a riverboat and I was hoping you might have seen them." The speaker accepted the tintype, looked at it, passed it to his companions, but blank stares showed on their faces.

"Haven't seen 'em," said one of the others, "Why you lookin'? They in trouble?"

Eli grinned, "No, I just have a message from their mother. They've been gone a couple years, worked on riverboats on the Missouri, done some panning in the goldfields, a little bit of everything. I've been a little late wherever I've been."

"Well, we're on the *Forty-Nine,* Captain Leonard White. We've been runnin' up to LaPorte and back. Ain't seen nuthin' of 'em."

"Thanks, men. Enjoy your breakfast," replied Eli as he started back to his table.

Donna came to the table, refilled his coffee cup, and sat down beside him. "Any luck?" she asked.

"Nope. But their boat has been going upstream to LaPorte and from what I heard, the twins were on a boat that went downstream with a big load of cargo. I thought they'd be back this way before now, but…" he shrugged.

## Chapter 33

## Interval

The buggy rattled and creaked as they rode from town. The afternoon was warm, the air cool, and the company exceptional. Donna leaned against Eli, her hand through his arm and her cheek on his shoulder when he asked, "Alright now, you'll have to tell me where we're going."

She giggled and answered, "With our lives, or for the day?"

"You know what I mean, today, now, right this moment. I'm not making plans for the future." He chuckled as she pulled herself close to him, and he added, almost in a whisper, "Not right yet, anyway."

She pointed ahead, "There. Where the road skirts the trees, there's a turnout and a nice clearing just past the trees. We can leave the buggy there, and we'll walk the rest of the way."

———

SHE LAY OUT THE BLANKET, opened the basket, and began arranging the various foodstuffs, giving access to each for both. Eli was stretched out, legs crossed at the ankles, and leaning on one elbow, watching Donna make her preparations. She was a beautiful woman, mature yet somewhat impulsive, well-kept and had all the right curves in all the right places. Eli grinned as she worked, thinking about her and the way her womanliness shaped her life. He remembered her willingness to use what would be considered by most as a man's weapon, and with her spirit and determination, she took no guff from any man. She was the kind of woman to walk beside a man and a woman that he could always depend upon.

Although they both had been married before, their lives with others had been less than complete. Eli remembered his wife, Margaret, and the times they had together, few though they were, and the family. They had spent little time with his family, more with hers, but little time together. She had been the wife of his good friend, Ferdinand Paine, and when he lay dying in his arms, he bid Eli to promise to take care of her. It was on this promise that he married her while she was pregnant with twins from her husband. But his career in the army gave them little time together and they never had the life of a family.

Donna's marriage had been one more of convenience than love, although she said she loved her husband, she did not respect him and his loose ways with gambling and more. She was relieved when he was killed and that allowed her to turn her life around and focus on her future rather than his dreams. Now with her business, it seemed she had found her place in life, at least for now, but he knew she was also very much interested in having a life together with him. He grinned as she kept looking back at him as she arranged everything, then sat back, her full skirt fanned out over her crossed legs, reminding him of the ceramic dolls featured in business windows in the big cities.

She smiled coyly at him, and asked, "Would you ask the Lord's blessing on the meal and on our time together?"

He nodded, sat up, and with head bowed, began a simple prayer of thanksgiving for the time together, the bounty, and the beautiful country around them. At the 'Amen,' Donna echoed the word and flounced about, starting to fill Eli's plate with the sumptuous feast. She handed it over and he sat with crossed legs, putting his plate on his lap and the glass of lemonade beside his leg. He sat the plate aside, stripped off his jacket and lay it aside, then with a touch of renewed vigor, set about devouring the feast.

Donna watched, taking pleasure in the man enjoying her handiwork in the kitchen. He was working on a tasty breast of fried chicken when she giggled at his antics. He paused, looked at her with a questioning expression, and asked, "Whaaat?"

She giggled, "Oh nothing. I just enjoy watching you enjoying the food I fixed for you. It gives a woman a special satisfaction to know you like what I've done!"

He grinned and continued with his feast. When he finished off the breast, he pulled the plate closer and started work on the potato salad, beans, and corn. He looked at her, "It's been a long time since I had a feast like this! Fried chicken, potato salad, corn, all fresh from the farm—it's great!"

She smiled, "That's what's so great about the area. Those farmers 'tween here and Wallula have everything —chickens for eggs and fried chicken, pigs for bacon and roasts, cows for milk and cheese and more, and beef cows for steaks. All the fresh vegetables you can ask for and more. But especially the fruit for pies, mmmm, they're the best!"

"Pies?" asked a grinning Eli, looking at the basket beside Donna.

She giggled, "Pie, just one."

———

THEY WALKED hand in hand along the shore, sat down on the bank, and at Donna's suggestion, took off their shoes to walk in the water. The rocks on the shoal were warmed by the sun, and they cautiously walked to water's edge. Donna, holding her skirt just above her ankles, put her toe in the water, and squealed, "It's cold!" and shivered, but left her foot in the water. She motioned to Eli who stepped beside her, giving her his arm to hold onto, then with pants legs rolled up, he stepped into the water, stood looking at her, "What? This ain't cold!"

They laughed at and with one another, Donna giggling, as they splashed through the shallows then back onto the warm rocks to the bank and sat down to dry off their feet and put shoes back on their cold feet. They laughed all the while, kidding one another, until she turned and leaned forward to plant a kiss on Eli's lips. His eyes flared, but as she leaned against him, he fell back, and she came with him.

She started to kiss him again until she heard a raspy voice come from the trees, "Wal! Whadda we have here? Ain'tchu bein' a little brazen there, girl?" laughed a whiskery faced man as he and another pushed through the trees, both holding rifles before them. The talker had long, stringy hair, a bulbous red nose, and tobacco stains streaming through the whiskers. His soiled shirt strained at the buttons above his belt and black belly hair showed in the gap. He laughed and his belly bounced as he leaned his head to his partner, "What'chu think, Skunk?"

The partner cackled, showing the sum of his three stained teeth, "Hehehehe—but that's the way I like 'em, Rufus!" He was half a head shorter than his partner and fifty pounds lighter, but it wasn't for the dirt he wore in his ragged and soiled attire.

Rufus looked at the two who were coming to their feet, Eli holding the checkered cloth napkin over the crook of his elbow, hiding his holstered Colt. Rufus said, "Now, you jist lift that there pistol from the holster real careful like, don' wan' it goin' off and hurtin' somebody now, do we?"

Eli complied, dropping the handkerchief and with two fingers and his thumb, carefully lifted the Colt, raised his eyebrows in a question and looked at the man. Rufus added, "Just drop it right thar," motioning with the muzzle of his rifle. As he moved, Eli noticed the rifle's hammer was not cocked, knowing the Spencer had to have the hammer cocked in a separate action before it would fire. A glance to the one called Skunk showed he was even more complacent and had dropped the rifle to his side.

Eli nodded, tossed the Colt to a patch of grass nearby, knowing the men would follow the pistol with their eyes, and that second was what he wanted. As he tossed the Colt with his left hand, he snatched the LeMat from his back with his right hand and brought it around, cocking it in the same motion and barked, "Drop 'em!" he ordered with the voice of command.

The two men looked with wide eyes, starting to lift

their rifles, but the LeMat barked and took Rufus in the upper chest. Skunk glanced to his partner, shouted, "No! No! Don't shoot!" and dropped his rifle as he lifted his hands.

Eli said, "Step back," motioning with his pistol.

The weasel-looking scoundrel snarled, glared at Eli, "You kilt him! He din't hurt you, why'd you kill 'im?" The words came out as more of a whine, pleading for reprieve.

Eli asked, "Where's your horses?"

"Back yonder. We heard you'ns splashin' in the water and Rufus thot we might fin' some women and thot we'd have some fun wit' 'em. We come through the trees, that's when we saw you. We weren't gonna do nuthin' bad, just have a li'l fun, you know," he shrugged, thinking Eli would believe him. Skunk appeared to relax, started to lower his arms as Eli moved closer to the dropped rifle.

Eli held the LeMat pointed to the rat-faced rogue, glanced at the rifle to kick it away. When he dropped his eyes, Skunk did just as Eli expected and reached for a knife that showed above his boot top. As he grabbed the haft, Eli dropped the hammer on the LeMat, the bullet shattered the sternum of the man causing Skunk to try to suck wind, wide eyes of disbelief staring at Eli. The impact of the slug drove him back off his feet and he stumbled, fell to his back, choked on his blood, and turned to the side to puke blood and sputum, gasped his last and lay still.

The blasts of the shots reverberated through the trees and the sounds of nature; birds, squirrels, and more, fell silent. The chuckle of the river behind them continued unabated as if carrying the story of the futility of man and how soon dreams, hopes, ambitions, and plans are silenced in an instant.

Eli looked at Donna who stood, handkerchief in hand, hand to her mouth, as she looked at the still forms of the two men who had designs on her just moments before and those thoughts had paralyzed her with fear. Although she had faced similar encounters, the drastic difference in just a moment of thought, from love to evil, had filled her with dread. She looked at Eli, took the three steps to him and wrapped her arms around him, putting her head on his chest, and sobbed.

He held her tight until her sobs stilled and spoke softly. "Let's get our things and go back to town. We'll need to tell the sheriff about this, and he can have someone take care of things."

She nodded her head against him, and he walked her to the buggy, helped her aboard, and returned to gather their things. They rode in silence as the buggy rattled on the road and town loomed ahead. Eli took her to the boardinghouse, saw her inside, then went to the sheriff's office, reported what happened and where, and took the buggy back to the livery. His mind was taking him in every direction—past, present, future, and more. Thoughts of Donna and his sons seemed to clash in his mind, especially when remembrances of his life before and since Margaret crowded in, clamoring for attention. He remembered his promise and walked back to the hotel.

# CHAPTER 34

## NEWS

The crowd had thinned after the midday meal and Eli sat reading an old copy of the *Walla Walla Statesman* newspaper with his back to the window, when Donna came to his table and sat beside him. She pulled the paper down to look at him, smiled, "Is there really anything that interesting in that paper?"

Eli chuckled, "Well, it says here that the teamsters are offering to haul freight for thirty-five dollars a ton, and Mr. John Allman got the contract to deliver mail between Walla Walla and Missoula City. Spokane had a fire in the carpenter shop of J. W. Smith, and in Benton, Montana, a bunch of Pend d'Orielle Indians ran off five head of horses." He paused, flipping the paper, and looked at Donna, "Other'n that, ain't much!"

She smiled at him, laughed, and reached for his hand. "Sheriff say much?"

"Nope. Said he knew 'em, glad they were done for, and asked if I wanted to pay for their buryin'. I said nope. He said, alright then. And we went our separate ways."

"Nothin' else?" asked Donna, her forehead wrinkled, as if she expected more.

"Well, he suggested I take over as sheriff so he could go look for gold."

"And...?"

"I said I have another job, lookin' for my sons."

Donna slowly lifted her head to nod, but the rattle of the front door pushing open caught her attention. She rose from her seat to greet the customers, "Hello, gentlemen. Have a seat and I'll fetch you some coffee!"

"Thank you, ma'am," answered the man in the lead. There were four men and Eli guessed by their attire and manner they were from a riverboat. He waited until Donna had given them cups and poured the coffee, taken their orders, and started to the kitchen. The men were jovial and laughing, looking about.

Eli rose and went to their table, "Howdy, gents! Mind if I ask you a question?"

The four men grew silent, looked at Eli with a questioning frown, and the previous speaker said, "Depends..."

Eli grinned, reached to his inside pocket of his jacket, and withdrew the tintype. He handed it to the leader, "Those are my sons, twins. I've been looking for them and had word they had taken a job on a riverboat. Thought you might have seen them."

"What makes you think we're from a riverboat?" asked one of the other men, watching his friend examine the tintype.

Eli grinned, nodded to one man, "Well, his Monmouth cap," to another, "his breeches," and to the questioner, "your dropped shoulder shirt. Those are common clothes of sailing vessels and since we're a long way from the ocean, I thought maybe you were on a riverboat."

As Eli spoke, the men looked at one another, the speaker nodded, and handed the tintype to another. "What's their names?"

"Jubal and Joshua Paine, they're my stepsons and I have a message from their mother."

The speaker looked to the others, received a slight nod from two, and turned back to Eli, "Yeah, we seen 'em. They were on the riverboat, *Oneonta*, Captain McNulty, with us. But they left."

Eli frowned, "Left?"

"Yeah, when we stopped at the Cascades to offload freight to portage, they left."

"Do you know where they went?"

"No, but the captain would. He talked to 'em a lot, got real friendly with 'em. He wasn't surprised when they left so we thought he knew all about it."

Eli was elated, but hesitant, "The captain in town?"

"Don't think so. He was still on the boat when we left, said he was waitin' for some more freight. We don't hafta be back till tomorrow."

Donna had come to the table with their orders, heard the last of the conversation, and looked at Eli as he said his thanks to the men and looked at her with a slow smile splitting his face. "They were on the boat with these men, but they left." He turned to look at the men again as they were starting to eat, "How long ago was that, when they left, I mean?"

The speaker looked at the others, back to Eli, "Oh, 'bout ten days, two weeks, I reckon. Kinda lose track o' time on the boat."

Eli nodded, "Thanks again, men." He looked at Donna and they walked back to his table together.

She sat beside him, scooted closer, "So, what're you gonna do?"

"I think I need to go to the dock at Wallula and talk to the captain. Dependin' on what he has to say, then I'll decide."

"You won't do anything without talking to me, will you?" pleaded Donna.

"Of course not. If I leave right away, I should make it by mornin'. Talk to him, return, maybe by late tomorrow. Then I'll come and we'll talk," explained Eli. He rose from his seat, as did Donna, and they walked outside to stand on the boardwalk.

They embraced, and Eli turned to leave, but Donna said, "I'll put together some food for you. Stop here 'fore you go." Eli nodded and went to the livery to saddle Rusty and get on the road.

———

By nightfall, Eli was on the road that hugged the north side of the Walla Walla River. He had ridden into the sun and watched it paint the western sky as it tucked itself away for the day. Dusk had offered ample light for a little more than an hour, and he pointed Rusty to the river for a break and a bite to eat. He loosened the girth, let Rusty graze on the grassy bank, and sat on a rock to dig into the bag prepared by Donna. Two thick roast beef sandwiches were wrapped in newspaper, and he opted for one with a big pickle and some water, sharing part of the sandwich with Lobo who refused to leave his side.

As the three-quarter moon hung in the eastern sky, the stars lit their lanterns, and Eli's night vision allowed him to mount up again and take to the trail. It was a quiet night and he let Rusty have his head while Eli slipped into his practice of prayer. He passed a few farms with lights aglow in the tall windows while dark shadows lay beside the buildings. It was a serene scene and one that prompted Eli to thoughts of home and hearth. He shook himself back to his present purpose and watched a big badger waddle across the road before them. He chuckled, reached down to stroke the neck of Rusty, and looked below at Lobo who stayed near the front legs of the big stallion.

As they continued their journey, Eli listened to the questions of a big barn owl, the ribbits of frogs, and the clattering of crickets. These were the sounds of the night and although somewhat haunting, they were also comforting, even the distant bark and cry of the coyotes. Rusty did a stutter step, looked with wide eyes and pricked ears into the grassy flats away from the course of the river and Eli spotted a lynx giving chase to an elusive and tricky jackrabbit, but the rabbit lost the race and the lynx sat on his haunches, the carcass of the big rabbit in his teeth as he looked about before beginning his feast.

For the rest of the night, the only creature Eli saw was a fat porcupine waddling across the road to disappear into the brush. As the moon lowered in the western sky, Eli nudged Rusty to the riverbank for another rest and some breakfast. This time he would fix some coffee to go with the offerings in the bag from Donna.

———

IT WAS APPROACHING midday when Eli rode up to the docks at Wallula. Two riverboats were moored but he was only interested in the larger of the two, the *Oneonta*. He drew Rusty to a halt beside a stack of freight, stepped down and ground tied the big stallion, pointed sternly to

Lobo and told him to stay with Rusty, then started to the plank at the prow of the boat.

Eli saw a man standing on the upper deck, watching him come near, and Eli looked up, shaded his eyes, and called out, "Permission to come aboard, sir?"

"Come ahead on," replied the man who stood with the usual captain's cap, white shirt over dark trousers and leaned on the rail with his elbows. Eli quickly mounted the steps and came forward to the captain who turned to look at his visitor.

Eli extended his hand to shake as he introduced himself, and added, "You're Captain McNulty?"

"That's right. You say your name was McCain?" replied the captain.

"Eli, Captain," responded Eli, reaching for the tintype. He handed it to the captain, "Those are my sons, Jubal and Joshua Paine. I understand they were with you when you went downriver, is that right?"

The captain looked at the tintype, up to Eli, and said, "I had a couple crew that looked like these two, but their names weren't McCain."

Eli grinned. "They're my stepsons. I have a message from their mother and was hoping to find them. I talked to some of your crew in town and they remembered the boys being a part of your crew."

"That's right. Good men too. Coulda used 'em on the return trip, but they had other ideas," suggested the captain.

Eli frowned, "Could you tell me about those ideas?"

The captain scowled, cocked his head to the side, and asked, "They're not in trouble?"

"No, like I said, just have a message for them."

"They tol' me 'bout desertin' the army, said they was

afraid you'd turn 'em in," stated the captain, giving Eli a squinting look waiting for an explanation.

Eli grinned, turned to lean on the rail, "I was a career officer for the Union, they deserted. We didn't have much of a family life, movin' around and all, so they probably thought I'd do something like that, but the message I have for them is that their mother passed but wanted them to go home to the family farm and make a life there. I promised her I'd do my best to find them and convince them to do just that. But..." he shrugged as he turned to look at the captain.

The captain leaned back against the rail, handed Eli the tintype, "I have a son, almost growed, and I've been almighty worried about his wild ways, so I think I know a little about how you might feel." He paused, looking about, and continued, "I liked your boys, talked with 'em a lot. They said they'd like to get a job on a boat, maybe go downriver to Portland, Vancouver, maybe get a job there. I told 'em about Captain Wolf of the *Wilson G. Hunt*, a boat that travels from the Cascades down to the mouth and back. But they also expressed interest in going on down the Columbia, maybe signing on with a schooner or something like that, said something about their father's family in shipping and that you had gone before the mast when you were young."

Eli grinned, shook his head, looked at the captain, "Yeah, I did, and talked about it when I was with the boys when they were, oh, twelve, thirteen, or so. They were wide-eyed with the stories I told, and I could see the excitement in their eyes. Never thought they'd wanna do that, though." He turned to look to the shore and the rolling hills beyond, shook his head and turned to the captain, "You have any ideas about ships and such that might moor at the mouth of the Columbia, you know, something that might appeal to the boys?"

"No, I don't. If you've been to sea, you know the ports are sometimes chosen by the weather and such, and depending on the possible cargo that could be taken on for distant ports. Your guess would be as good as mine," replied the captain. "I don't envy you, it must be hard, not knowing about your boys, I mean."

Eli sighed heavily, his shoulders lifted with the deep breath, turned around, "Reckon I'll have to give it some thought, pray about it, think a lot, then try to come up with a plan or something." He turned back, looked to the captain, extended his hand to shake, "Thanks, Captain. I appreciate the information. You've been a help."

"You're welcome, Eli. I hope and pray you find your boys. You might do just as well stayin' in one place, maybe go back to your family's business, or their mother's farm, and just wait for them to show up, they're bound to, sooner or later."

"That's just it, there's nothing certain, and I made a promise to my wife. But where I go from here, I just don't know." With a nod, he went to the stairs, lifted his hand to say goodbye, and departed the boat. He swung aboard Rusty, motioned for Lobo to follow, and started back to Walla Walla. The grey packhorse was at the livery, and he promised Donna he would return to let her know what was planned, but as the big claybank stallion ambled on the trail, his usual long-legged gait stretched him out. Eli lapsed into his thoughts, wondering about the future, remembering the past, and thinking of the twins.

Would he ever find them? Would he ever fulfill the covenant made with his wife? He lifted his eyes to Heaven and called out to God, "I need you, Lord. What do I do now, where do I go, and what about my future, home, family, and more? I guess I just don't understand."

As he rode and prayed, he was reminded of one of his favorite passages, *Trust in the Lord with all thine heart; and lean not unto thine own understanding. In all thy ways acknowledge him, and he shall direct thy paths.* Proverbs 3:5-6. He smiled at the thought and the remembrance, chuckled to himself, and added to his prayer, "Alright, alright. I'll trust you."

# A Look at: Rocky Mountain Saint

## The Complete Christian Mountain Man Series

**Best-selling western author B.N. Rundell takes you on a journey through the wilderness in this complete 14-book mountain man saga!**

Holding on to the dream of living in the Rocky Mountains that Tatum shared with his father, he begins his journey—a journey that takes him through the lands of the Osage and Kiowa and ultimately to the land of the Comanche. Now he has a family, and the wilderness makes many demands on anyone that tries to master the mountains…

*"Rundell's Rocky Mountain Saint series is marvelous and inspiring." –* **Reader**

Follow Tate Saint, man of the mountains, on his journey from boyhood to manhood where he faces everything from the wilds of the wilderness to forces of nature and historic wars.

*Rocky Mountain Saint: The Complete Series includes – Journey to Jeopardy, Frontier Freedom, Wilderness Wanderin', Mountain Massacre, Timberline Trail, Pathfinder Peril, Wapiti Widow, Vengeance Valley, Renegade Rampage, Buffalo Brigade, Territory Tyranny, Winter Waifs, Mescalero Madness and Dine' Defiance.*

### *AVAILABLE NOW*

# About the Author

Born and raised in Colorado into a family of ranchers and cowboys, **B.N. Rundell** is the youngest of seven sons. Juggling bull riding, skiing, and high school, graduation was a launching pad for a hitch in the Army Paratroopers. After the army, he finished his college education in Springfield, MO, and together with his wife and growing family, entered the ministry as a Baptist preacher.

Together, B.N. and Dawn raised four girls that are now married and have made them proud grandparents. With many years as a successful pastor and educator, he retired from the ministry and followed in the footsteps of his entrepreneurial father and started a successful insurance agency, which is now in the hands of his trusted nephew. He has also been a successful audiobook narrator and has recorded many books for several award-winning authors. Now finally realizing his life-long dream, B.N. has turned his efforts to writing a variety of books, from children's picture books and young adult adventure books, to the historical fiction and western genres which are his first love.

Printed in Great Britain
by Amazon

26311090R00138